Kristin found the mare for sale at the County Fair. It took some time to convince her family that she was responsible enough to own a horse, but they finally agreed to give her the chance. That first summer with Blueberry was beautiful for Kristin. With the help of her best friend, Danny Wasilewski, the warm days flew by in training, schooling, and just enjoying Blueberry.

The winter, though, was another matter. Danny was sent away to live with his uncle, and Kristin's father's prejudice against her friend did not help her to overcome the loss.

Kristin also faced a struggle to hold her beloved Blueberry—a struggle which depended on so many things: school grades, the work about the farm, and, most of all, her acceptance of the obligations that accompany maturity. It was also up to Kristin to help Danny in his flight from the law and to prove to her father that the son of a gypsy could not only be proud, but honest and worthwhile.

BLUEBERRY

BLUEBERRY

By

Helga Sandburg

THE DIAL PRESS   NEW YORK   1963

For my daughter
Karlen Paula

My beautiful, my beautiful,
That standest meekly by,
With thy finely arched and glossy neck
And thy dark and fiery eye!

—*The Arab and His Steed*
Caroline Norton

BLUEBERRY

❧ ❧ ❧ **I** ❧ ❧ ❧

The row started

at the supper table when Daddy saw her math grade: D. "I'm no good at arithmetic," the littlest sighed, "but I got B in English."

And Mother asked, "Did you remember to water your guinea pigs today?"

And Margo said, "Daddy, Kristin didn't, and their pans were dry."

And Astrid giggled, "Our Kristin ought to have a camel and it wouldn't matter when she always forgets."

Kristin shook her head. "Everyone picks on me. I hate being the baby of this family."

And Daddy said, "I think you girls should take Kristin's pigs to the fair in the morning and sell every one if you can find a buyer."

And Kristin stared at him stunned. "No. That's not fair. I forgot this one time! Margo," she told her sister, "I hate you for this."

And Margo said, "No, Daddy, that's no way to do. Give Kristin another try. I vote for it. How do the rest of you stand?"

Everyone but Daddy was affirmative so her pets were safe, but then the subject of her grades came up again, and then Danny was knocking on the door. "Hey, Kristin," he called, "can you come play!" Summer vacation was beginning today.

Daddy scraped back his chair. "I'll get that. You stay at the table."

She leaned over to pull on her sneakers, discarded during the scene, under her chair. She heard his tone which meant the law would be laid down shortly. In a painful way she got up. "No."

And Margo told her, "Daddy said stay."

And Kristin said, "You shut up."

And Mother protested, "Dears," stroking her cat.

And they all rose and followed her to the doorway. Daddy's temper was loose; he began yelling, "Run along. I don't want her playing with you. School's out and don't come around here. If you don't stay away, I'll go see your dad and make it clear. Let Kristin alone during this summer!"

Danny stood in the same kind of shock as Kristin. He hadn't known how Daddy felt and she hadn't told him. His mouth fell open. He flushed and didn't dare look at any of the family and walked away.

"Gypsy," Daddy muttered and looked at Kristin. "And see that you mind. Your fourteenth birthday is past; you're not to go over to those Poles' farm to visit either. I'll hear no excuse, not one." He marched away to get his hammer to put up the new awnings, the eyes of his four women upon him with varying degrees of approval.

Kristin had kept her teeth gritted, and she nodded, unable to say a word. Her eyes were hot and blue like violets so that later Astrid whispered, "I could see how mad you were by your eyes, baby!" As soon as Daddy had gone she ran like crazy for the soft grass behind the goat barn and hurled herself upon it, cast into the depths of gloom. No one could comfort Kristin when she was really blue that way, not Astrid or Margo or even Mother. Maybe sometimes Danny. But both her sisters came to try; they stood over her.

After a while Astrid stopped patting her shoulder, and Margo said, "Come on in the barn while we milk the goats and we'll talk about it."

But Kristin shouted, "Go away. I hate everybody." And they knew she meant it and left. Brooding, she wandered up to her room and got her swim suit.

There was a chill in the air as the twilight made itself ready. It was quarter of eight and the sun was setting. She went down the long gravel road, over the cooling sand, and in twenty minutes reached the great lake. It was choppy and the whitecaps broke churning. There was just enough undertow to make it interesting. She was alone on the shore; she found a flat driftwood board and rode it in on the waves.

"Ho, horse," she shouted and was hurled by the last breaker upon the bank, holding her breath while the water covered her. She scrambled to her feet, her long blond braids soaked. "Good boy, good horse!" She saw the tall silver stallion, not the gray piece of wood. She centered her mind upon the comfort of the dream and away from the way Daddy had acted.

The dunes loomed, dusky, above Lake Michigan, bordering it. The pines that crowded upon the sand hills swept their arms in the windy air; they held nesting birds and from them the young ones made their first flights. Sparse grasses grew uneasily in the barren ground, smothered by the grains as the wind shifted or drying out as their roots were uncovered. They refused to perish entirely until their last root tendril was torn up. In a storm,

sometimes, they blew away in the wind accompanied by
tumbleweeds and spray from the raging water nearby. The
shapes of the dunes varied from season to season as the
wind shoved the sand about; it was said that the hills
walked. It was a strange bleak country, bitter cold in
winters when the winds came flying out of the north
across the lake; it was hot as Egypt in summers.

Inland the soil grew gradually richer, until a mile or
less from the lake it supported orchards and vineyards.
Peaches, apples, nectarines, pears, apricots, cherries, plums
and grapes; currants, raspberries, dewberries, boysenberries;
fabulous, flowing like honey from trees and vines and
bushes, they filled crates and baskets and were carted by
trucks to cities and canneries.

Kristin was pulling on the canvas shoes she'd left on
the shore; her arms and legs had goosebumps as she
climbed the dune fronting the lake. For good luck she
began counting the last of the evening's sailing gulls:

> *One for sorrow, two for joy,*
> *Three for a present, four for a letter,*
> *Five for something better!*

There were eight of the prophetic birds and it came out
three for a present, which wasn't bad. The dune dipped
sharply into a deep blow like a little valley, and she followed
the long sandy trail, and up the next dune, and finally
leading over a creek-bridge which bordered the run-down
Wasilewski farm. The orchard trees were broken and almost too old to bear any more, the barns shabby and
leaky-roofed, the house gray with great shaggy lilacs and
syringas about the windows and doors, shadowing the
interior, making it for a few months of the year fragrant
with their bloom.

In the almost-dark she could see Danny finishing some work, kneeling over a furrow, an ancient straw hat on his head, his shirt off. At fourteen he wasn't filled out yet and his shoulder blades stuck out. His dad, balding and bent, was coming out of an old shed, bringing a basket of seedlings.

Kristin intended to slip down and see Danny now and then, if she pleased, despite Daddy's edict. She hailed the two with a shout as she passed along the farm fence. The older man never could have run the farm at all if it weren't for Danny. The heart had gone out of Mr. Wasilewski; the place barely made them a living at truck-cropping though they'd once managed pretty well when there was a woman.

The man waved back at the girl in the bathing suit. Danny, his bare knees in the plowed earth, grinned, acknowledging her rebellion against Daddy; he swung his straw hat. His curls were close-cropped and his eyes soft and dark. His ragged jeans were cut short; in summers his clothes would become tattered until they nearly dropped from him, though he dressed pretty decently in the school season. He'd been riding with Kristin on the same bus since first grade.

Kristin took a handful of green peas from the basket on the fruit and vegetable stand by the propped-open wood Wasilewski gate. On the counter were heaped leaf lettuce and radishes, washed and stacked, and green and white slim onions, baskets of whatever they pulled out of the rows or plucked from green stems. She followed the road which went on a mile further inland, shelling the peas and chewing their sweetness as she walked.

By the time she reached Highway 12 it was dark. Daddy was still hammering on the new awnings of the

Blue Coffee Kettle, which served travelers and on occasional nights, nearby residents. The electric lights were bright on the old-fashioned broad porch that ran around three sides of the house. In the morning, as he did at every season's start, Daddy would paint afresh the pot-shaped blue sign which swung between two white posts beside the four-lane pavement.

"It's dark, Kristin," he shouted. "Where've you been?"

"I don't know," she yelled back, "I'm going to bed."

"Dry your hair before you sleep on it so you don't catch cold. And hang your suit on the line; don't leave it on the floor." Assertive as the littlest, he reached for another handful of tacks.

Kristin let the door slam behind her without reply. Mother's whistling from the kitchen rang out upon the hammer strokes that came now uninterrupted. Mother was in the kitchen with two neighbor women who waited table and dishwashed and did whatever else was needed. The restaurant specialized in a Scandinavian buffet, offered nightly in summers, and was noted for its Swedish coffee. Mother never let a filter enter her kitchen, and she used raw egg whites to settle the grounds. Kristin climbed the stairs; she was all tired out. She threw her swim suit in the corner and flopped down, her braids dampening the pillow with lake water.

She awoke in the morning to the same whistle and song from the kitchen below, coming over the chatter of the just-arrived waitresses. Kristin went to sit in the kitchen on a stool, eating cornflakes and feeling blue; she didn't know why; sometimes she was and sometimes she wasn't. Her sisters were busy as bees, but all Kristin could do was listen to Mother and spoon the cereal.

You ride the billy goat
And I'll ride the mule;
First one gets to heaven's
Going to sit in the cool!

Behind the house were two acres of land which pastured nearly thirty head of purebred Nubian goats: milk does, bucks and kids; and where three-tiered rabbit hutches and a dog house and a long low barn and various tool and garden sheds spread out, where vegetable rows and flower plots were tenderly cared for. Astrid, almost seventeen, was raising fancy vegetables, using special fertilizers; and Margo, eighteen, was pampering seedling pansies with a netting of ripped sheets that she strung over the tiny green things. The pair hoped to cop some prizes at the Tri-County Fair held late in the summer every year, around Labor Day.

The older girls and Mother were animal-and-garden-crazy. Daddy'd had a half-ton of horse manure dumped by the garden beds for a special present once; it had been Mother's birthday but everyone thanked him.

Today a little county fair was going on about six miles away, and Astrid and Margo had finished the milking early. They were loading their entries: long-eared varied-colored Nubians, rabbits picked from Astrid's Flemish Giants, a pair of Muscovy ducks, a trio of Margo's banty chickens. There was a single entry from their little sister: an Abyssinian guinea pig that she'd been given for her fourteenth birthday a couple of months ago; it was shipped clear from a California cavy breeder Margo knew about.

Before they drove off in Daddy's two-door Ford, the trailer behind bedded with straw, Astrid dashed down into the cellar for some jars of tomato jam and grape jelly and

watermelon preserve that she'd put up last year. Then
Margo went to the garden to throw together a few flower
arrangements; every year they got prizes for their entries
which, giggling, they would assemble at the very last possible instant.

Margo directed the littlest who came out of the
kitchen to see them off, "Watch Sophie, Kristin. She was
due to kid yesterday." Margo always spoke as if the world
were her special property.

Astrid sat at the wheel, her round face soft. From the
crate on the floor in back the Muscovy ducks whispered
their alarm together. "Darn it, don't go off and forget,
baby."

The three sisters were blue-eyed and blond but none
looked alike. Kristin had thick ropes of braids which came
to the belt of her boy's blue jeans. She had a strong body
and wide small hands. "What'll you bring me?"

Margo raised her eyebrows; her lap and arms were full
of flowers. She was petite, her hair in a high bun, and wear-
ing an orange sheath dress. Kristin hated the way Margo
was nowadays and they had good fights sometimes. Margo
tried to be grown-up though she was only four years older
than Kristin, which latter fact Kristin shouted upon
Margo's deaf ears at every opportunity. "We'll get you a
surprise," Margo said. "Now, let's get going!"

"Turn the dogs loose when we're out of sight," Astrid
told Kristin, and winked, comradely, shifting gears.

Off they went, the dust flailing from the stoned drive,
and down the smooth highway. The goats baaed to Kristin
from the screened rear of the trailer as they caught sight
of her lone figure left behind. She called, "Take care of
Teddy. And if you see a good guinea pig female, buy it and
I'll pay you back!" Her words were lost in the motor noise.
She wasn't exactly enthusiastic about the guinea pigs, but

they were better than nothing. She felt too, that they were a test the family had contrived to try Kristin's dependability. Once she'd had a few white mice which she forgot to feed for a whole week and they died. Kristin never quite lived that down though she was only seven at the time.

She sighed and wandered to the little barn; the morning air was still cool; a light breeze blew from the lake, as the air, chilled by the cold water, was drawn in to the quickly-heated land.

As she opened the barn door the dogs rose in the dusky interior. Kristin didn't even have a dog of her own, while Astrid had a pair of young Irish setters, and Margo had Bimbo, an elderly collie. Kristin felt how her sisters owned thousands of pets, and all she had were four guinea pig females and Teddy, the new male. And, of course, there was Smoky, whom she adored, a gift of her dentist two years ago. Whining, the setters reared on her, leaving bits of straw on her old jersey. Bimbo, who was lame, stalked out to lie in the sun and wait on Margo's return.

Kristin unfastened the door to a wood cage nailed on the wall. Her dentist had shot Smoky's parents and the baby crow had been heard yelping in the nest. It hopped to her wrist. A shoelace thong hung from one leg. She went to the old huge tulip tree behind the goat quarters. The bird clung precariously, half-flapping, as she climbed the branches to the platform of boards nailed across two stout limbs. The canvas walls to the playhouse were by now holey and half-rotted. She crept under them and sat cross-legged in the haven spot, green branches repeating above her, reaching high. Smoky perched on the canvas-draped rail, button eyes alert. She reached a hand up and stroked the black glossy breast absently. The eyes followed her movement, the head bent, curious.

"You're silly." She frowned.

Her little creatures were sweet and she loved them.
But all her desire was for that great intelligent beast she'd
wanted all her life. Forever she'd made up daydreams about
how it would be. All the people in her household had what
they wanted. Even Mother had a great Blue Persian called
Mr. Shams, that roamed about the dining room, sniffing
the legs of customers, trailing Mother's heels as she made
up beds or dusted somewhere or sewed curtains. And Daddy
had his way; he joked that his four women were his pets.

The summer streamed out before Kristin in a huge
empty space of time. Every girl in the eighth grade, almost,
had been boy-crazy except for Kristin. She was famous for
being horse-crazy. Danny had a beat-up sidesaddle which
he'd let Kristin strap on a log when she was nine or ten.
Sometimes she felt half her life was spent at fantasies; nothing was real. In winters when she dragged her toboggan out
on the snow-deep dunes she still called it a golden mare,
whispering a name to herself. It was all imagining. She felt
fiercely that she ought to have the real thing.

She slipped the crow onto her shoulder again and
swung down to the ground easily, her hands sure upon the
gray limbs. She dropped the last six feet and the crow
winged ahead, lighting on a fence post to wait for her. It
opened its yellow mouth and squawked. She caught it up
on the run as she hurried to the pen where Sophie lay.

The doe was chewing her cud, placid. Her coat was
dark red, her ears, like heavy leaves, curved almost a foot
in length along her nose which was Egyptian and arched.
Her amber oval eyes viewed the girl cooly, reflective. Kristin put Smoky in his roost and came to scratch Sophie
about the ears so the doe turned and twisted her head
with pleasure. Kristin felt that when she was old enough
she'd get a job, if they'd let her. Maybe now that Margo

was going off to college in the fall, the school superintendent would hire Kristin to replace her as his office girl. But she knew that was a fiction too; Margo was efficient, a whiz at her studies. Kristin examined herself; even when her nails were just scrubbed her hands looked grubby; she was disorderly; her hair, just braided, straggled unkempt. She wondered if she'd ever grow up and inspire confidence.

She closed the pen gate behind her and ordered the red setters to lie down near Bimbo and not follow. She went off through the woods by the short cut to the Wasilewski farm. If she met Danny she didn't care; always it was the children against the adults. Both had their own mores, their own secrets, their own language. The countries were islands, separate, and one crossed the sea of division somewhere between nine and seventeen years old, depending on one's nature, on loneliness, on the maturing of bodies, on the wisdom of the elders.

Kristin paced swiftly over the path, feeling the snail's slowness of a two-legged human. Overhead in their peculiar island, birds were busy in the green sun-drenched leaves; mostly unseen they moved about, in their beaks, twigs for nests, or a grasshopper or butterfly, some food for an open-mouthed fledgling. A catbird squalled, raucous, and then dulcet-toned, went to warble from the top of a sycamore. Across the path stretched a new spider web, and Kristin paused to duck under it and then scan the shining strands for the minute animal. She caught it in her palm; she believed in trying everything; she told it:

> *If you want good luck today*
> *Let the spider get away!*

She'd knock on wood, spit over her shoulder, catch leaves when they drifted down to wish upon; she'd even put her sweater on backwards for luck when she took the crumby math final. Who knew what was false lore and what was true anyway? She put the spider back on its thread and it scuttled into the green shadow.

She entered the gray tumbling building, once a carriage house, the floor of packed dirt. On the walls were tacked half-torn carnival posters, thirty years old, one of a sixteen-year-old girl with long black hair, in a ballerina skirt, surrounded by a ring of eight galloping black stallions. The sun came pale through the dusty windows; in its path motes shimmered and quivered. Machinery stood rusty and unusable. Kristin gathered her saliva and spit the way Danny did, aiming for and missing a great yellow-brown wasp that fumbled at the glass, refusing to believe there was a barrier between itself and freedom.

Kristin reached up and unbuttoned the latch so the insect stepped long-legged into the day and disappeared. She sat on a pile of musty folded gunny sacks under the rack that held the ancient sidesaddle. She drew her knees to her chin and interlaced her fingers, and began working out a complex story involving danger and death, and always the hero horse who with her astride saved the situation.

The noon hour went by. Her parents never fussed if she missed breakfast or lunch. There was always food about the restaurant's kitchen, and the family was casual about the first two meals. Only at the evening table was she expected to sit with the others; that was the hour for discussion, decision, and manifestoes; for voting. Kristin seldom won a case which she attributed largely to being the baby of three sisters and thereby bullied. It was well into the afternoon when she remembered. She left the saddle on the tree and trotted homeward, fearful.

"Why do I always forget? Am I a dope!"

Sometimes she felt she was hopeless. There was a stitch in her side, but dogged she ran on, enduring the hurt. She could hear Margo already, *Daddy, I don't think Kristin knows what responsibility signifies.* And Astrid would kick her under the table and wink, trying to make her get the giggles. Kristin disliked them both as she swung around the bend into the barnyard, her guilt building.

Sophie had retreated and was in the darkened corner; Kristin squinted, unable to see the red animal after the blinding outside light. She heard the hoarse bawl and approached, quiet, to find a foreleg of the unborn kid had emerged but was dry, denoting that the labor had been going on a while. Kristin knelt over the doe, brushing off the straw stuck to the soft gelatinous tiny hoof. She put her sun-brown hand to Sophie who muttered over it and then licked it. Startled, the doe began to strain again. Kristin pushed the leg gently back into the passage, following it with her hand. Sophie groaned and threw herself on her side; Kristin felt about to locate the other hoof and to turn the head which had twisted backward, obstructing the journey out.

"Easy, girl." She felt how she would not hurry or panic while handling the doe. When alone, she knew sometimes a power like this; in the presence of others she was often confused. At school it was the same: she was okay when she studied the book, but when the history teacher spoke her name all she'd read disappeared in an instant. Now she was calm and careful, helping the laboring beast.

With the nose directed outward she held the legs by the fingers of her hand, dragging down when the doe pushed. The kid resisted and Kristin blamed herself for going off to have some fun. In a final agonized noise, the head and quickly the rest came out in a limp caul-slippery mass; the kid was red and white spotted. Sophie raised her head, blatting like a question, and Kristin moved the kid around to place it before her. It gave a little human baby's wail.

Then the dam was straining again and Kristin waited while the second, a black male, arrived quickly, head first. The doe got to her legs and began to clean her young. Kristin rubbed the newborn ones with a gunny sack; Sophie yawned the way goats do when in discomfort.

Kristin went to make a bran mash, mixing into the dry chaff molasses and hot water. Sophie dug into it greedily while the girl took the kids away to a box where the newborn ones were kept. She returned to milk out the first thick yellow colostrum from the doe who snuffled at her hair and washed her cheek, bawled after her as she went to feed it to the babies.

When the girls returned they praised her; they hadn't had time to get her present; they flung down two blues and a white ribbon for the flower arrangements. Animals were to be judged the next day and on the third day fowl and preserves would get their awards.

"Goat classes start at nine in the morning. Toggenburgs first, Nubians second, Saanens and Alpines last. Sheep and pigs are in the morning, too. In the afternoon horses and cattle." Margo had slipped into fresh denim shorts and was brushing Bimbo's white coat with slow strokes, removing the mats of hair from the brush bristles. They were in the back yard. "There's a horse show in the afternoon, Kristin."

"It's a rodeo," Astrid said. "I'll come back for you." She sat on the edge of the porch, her short flaxen hair mussed, her yellow dress rumpled, one of the new kids, the spotted doe, sprawled on her lap. It sucked on her finger. She put it down and it staggered and then gave a little sidewise jump and stumbled over the grass to Bimbo. The collie, used to the goats, licked it and stood indulgent while it nudged, instinctively seeking an udder in the fur.

"She's just what we wanted," Margo said.

"The right color too, baby," Astrid told Kristin.

"We'll have to slaughter the buck," Margo said. "No one wants a buck born after April."

"Don't think about it," Astrid sighed. "Think about naming the doe."

"What about calling her Sophronica," Margo said.

"Is that a made-up name?" Kristin was flat on her back on the lawn, the crow in the tree overhead. "Why not call her Spot? I dare you."

"Say, Kristin," Astrid looked over, "did you remember to wash your hands before you went after the kid?"

Kristin rose startled to her knees. "I forgot!"

"It doesn't matter," Margo said. "It doesn't signify anything. You saved the day." She shook her finger at Bimbo, coaxing him. "Be good; hold still. The poor thing thinks you're her mother."

Astrid started to giggle and tried to make Kristin join her. "Goofy old Bimbo!" She pushed her slipper toward Kristin sitting tensely in the grass.

But Kristin spoke in a rush, her blue eyes brilliant as the sun went down, looking as if she were backed into a corner and opposed the world. There was no hint of tears or self-pity as she confessed her wrong, "I don't want you to bring me a surprise. I won't take it if you do. I forgot about Sophie, and I just got back in time or that spotty kid would have died."

Amazed they watched the littlest walk away. "What's got into her now?"

❦ ❦ ❦ II ❦ ❦ ❦

At daylight in the

morning Kristin came into the barn where the girls were hurrying at their chores so they could get to the fair to tend the animals left there in the show stalls of the exhibition shed. Kristin was sleepy-eyed. "I'll help. What you want me to do?" She yawned.

"Throw down hay." Margo was seated at the raised wood milking stand stripping an udder, the white streams whining into the tiny steel bucket. The Nubian's slender neck was fastened by a stanchion; it nuzzled the grain in the pan before it, licked its favorite kernels of grain first.

"Okay." Kristin started toward the ladder to the loft.

"First clean out the old hay from the mangers," Astrid said.

Kristin pulled the alfalfa and lespedeza stalks from the alley that ran down the center of the barn where the goats ate; they'd nibbled off the tiny tender leaves and stems, disdaining the coarser parts. "What'll I do with it? The rabbits can't eat it all."

"Scatter it for bedding," Margo said. "Even the rabbits are getting spoiled and don't want it."

"There's more than enough to feed a horse." Kristin kicked the heap of green stuff to spread it on the spongy barn floor.

"Don't get started on that topic," the eldest said. "I'll put my hands over my ears."

"It's so rich," Kristin growled, "I wouldn't even have to buy grain."

"Tell Daddy; don't tell us!"

"Ugh," Kristin said, climbing the rungs to the loft from where her voice descended, faint. "Astrid, you come back and pick me up this aft, will you?"

"Okay; I'll be here about two."

Astrid distributed the hay tumbling through the loft chute. She opened the big sliding doors so the herd could roam out upon the field or return to the barn shade as they pleased. Then Margo hurried to the kitchen, clattering the milk pails; Kristin held the setters by their collars so they wouldn't chase the car, and her sisters were gone.

Kristin trudged down the road, spitting when cars passed and raised swirls of dirt. Her bare ankles were grimy and a fine sweat stood on her forehead as she reached the Wasilewski farm. Danny was tying pole beans to seasoned stakes he had cut in the woods last winter.

When Astrid drove into the *Blue Coffee Kettle*'s drive at two o'clock Kristin said, "Danny's going to be waiting at the bend."

"You better not," Astrid said.

"Why?"

"I heard Daddy tell you not to."

"But why!" She challenged her sister in a swaggering fashion, leaning back, her hands in her jeans pockets. "And don't tell on me."

Astrid shrugged. "Not me."

"And if *she* does, I won't watch when the next doe has kids." Kristin's fingers were on three dollar bills, enough to get both Danny and herself into the grandstand and buy

orange drinks and Baby Ruths, too. She wasn't afraid of
bossy Margo or Daddy either.

"The goat judge is so dumb this year," Astrid said.

"What'd you win?"

"We didn't have much luck except Rani took Best
Yearling class so we don't care. I don't know how this
judge ever passed her qualification exam; she's crazy over
size and doesn't know beans about conformation."

"What about Teddy?"

"He's the only Abyssinian guinea pig so he didn't get
anything. I took a blue on the rabbits, though. Best Pair."

"I might bring Teddy home tonight. I don't know why
I let you take him." Kristin felt her taut body like a spring.
If there was any kind of a riding contest she intended to get
into it. Last year she rode a mule bareback and got
bucked off. She was a lot bolder than her friend. "There
he is."

Sitting by the highway, cross-legged, he was chewing
grass. He clambered into the back seat. "Hi, Astrid."

"How's vacation, Danny?"

"Astrid won't tell," Kristin said. "And let us out before
we get to the grounds, so Margo doesn't see him, will you?"

"Don't be melodramatic, baby." Astrid's checkered
pastel frock contrasted with the two in jeans; Danny's top
a black jersey and Kristin's a blue farmer's shirt she'd
ordered from the Sears catalog. She let them out at the gate
ticket stand. "How are you getting home, Danny?"

"Hitching a ride."

"I'll pick you up here at six sharp, Kristin."

"Okay." Kristin's heavy braids were fastened at the
ends with rubber bands. She scorned ribbons and only for
special occasions like Margo's graduation would she con-

sent to combing her hair out and tying it back with a velvet band.

"I've got a dollar," Danny said, as she pulled out her bills for the tickets. "But save it for the rodeo."

"That's right; they charge extra."

Danny nudged her arm with an elbow. They were passing the sideshows, the Beautiful Fat Girl, the Snake Charmer, the Sword Swallower, Jojo The Wild Man; barkers hailed them and there was the tinkling of the merry-go-round. A Wild Himalayan Bear, scrubby and collar-marked, yawned as they paused before him. "My mother was with a carnival. She liked bears so much she saved one's life."

"I love it that your mother was a real gypsy!"

"A *gitana*. That's the Spanish way to say it. Did you know before she could marry my father, he had to get permission of the gypsy king?"

"I wonder what he's like."

"He has diamonds mounted in his teeth. And he wears an earring. My mother wore gold ones, and her lobes were pierced the week after her birth." Danny strutted. "The *crayí* didn't want her leaving the tribe."

"What about the bear?"

"They were crossing a river and the animal cage tipped over and fell in. The bear was locked in and my mother jumped right after and got his door open and came to shore with him."

"Wow." They left the animal who gazed after with half-closed lids.

"She couldn't swim and she told everyone the bear brought her in and saved her life."

"There's the rodeo," Kristin pointed. They hurried. Danny's mother had handled a horse act too when she was sixteen. She stood in the ring and snapped her fingers and eight stallions stopped running and came to face her.

Over the archway to the canvas tent was a listing of the attractions. Danny read off, "*Hurricane, The Biting Horse. Hates All Humanity. Ten Dollars To Anyone Who Can Catch Hold Of His Bridle.* Let's go take a look at what else they have."

"I hope there's a bucking contest this year."

There was, the second event, and Kristin along with others tried to stay on the flat saddle of the pony whose hair was long and shaggy, who threw his heels skyward as soon as the stirrup was touched. When she returned to the bench beside Danny, he said, "You can't win that one."

"Why?"

"He's trained for it. But I'll tell you about the act coming up, this Hurricane. I know of an act like it."

"Say!"

"You have to give him the right signal. They'll wait till everyone gets run out of the ring, and then the nag's trainer will go in and walk up and take his bridle."

An exhibition black bronco was holding a line taut while a skinny young man, his big hat still on, was tying the legs of a thrown calf together. He threw up his hands. He mounted and galloped around, waving his Stetson while an assistant freed the calf, and all disappeared at full speed through the entryway. The ringmaster was shouting through his megaphone.

"Folks! Here comes Hurricane!"

A small bay gelding, well-muscled, shot into the ring; he wore a red leather bridle, its loose reins were fastened to brass rings on a red belly-band. His face was dished; his mane was clipped and the tail roached halfway down, all of which accented his vicious look. Halting, wary, he switched his tail and waited. As the first farm boy dropped from the railing, reckless, disdaining the gate, the gelding's appearance changed: his ears went flat and he plunged in a streak, panther-like, reins taut, open-mouthed. The boy turned tail; the ringmaster continued his spiel.

"Have we another contestant? Why are you running, my friend! Hurricane used to be a mine pony, folks, until one day he hauled off and kicked a line of coal cars from the track and chased six men into a corner. They had to stay there till help came and lassoed him. That was the day this show came by and we took him on. We have to lay him down to get that red bridle on him you see there. One day he's going to take someone's arm off and the Humane Society's going to cart him away."

Another boy dropped in, and then a tall young tourist woman in slacks and sombrero called that she was willing. When the gelding galloped toward her she screamed and stumbled and two show hands held him off with shouts and waves until her boy friend retrieved her. The ringmaster was delighted; this was a nice area, not all country people but a spattering of resorters whose unconventionality was as entertaining sometimes as the fair itself to the farmers.

"Don't we have anyone else who wants to try for a nice crisp ten dollar bill? Do we have to make fools out of all you folks out there!"

Danny spoke to Kristin and she got up. "Mister."

Everyone's eyes turned on the girl going down the short dusty aisle. She wanted to turn back, anonymous, but she needed more to touch the horse. She slipped through the gate into the arena. The beast whirled about, spotting her figure; he flung his dark tail from side to side, then started his dash toward Kristin. She walked forward to meet him and somewhat bewildered, he slowed, shaking his head and lowering it, the long ears pricked. He let her come close.

She looked at the strange eyes, small in the dished face, the whites showing, the brown speckles in them. She was gesturing in a downward pushing movement with her left hand. "Hey, hey, horse." She felt the way she had when Sophie's kid was dry and she knew she must act without haste.

The gelding shied away in a sidewise lunge and trotted in a springy gait to the other end of the ring where he waited on the girl. She followed, "Easy. Hey, hey."

The horse seemed entranced as she took his bridle; she held the reins firmly under his chin, and while the crowd applauded, turned the horse and walked him out. In the passageway she stood half-lost.

Then the ringmaster was standing over her, rough. "Well, sweetheart? Think you're pretty smart?" He was red-faced under his battered derby, and there was no hint of a smile about him.

Danny was pelting up. "Kristin! I told you!" He laid his dark hand on the animal whose black skin quivered, and who shifted his legs nervously. Danny ignored the man except to cry, "Isn't it great?" He talked to the girl. "He's a natural for this act; he's the type would rather you let him alone than fuss around him. See his dish face and long ears; he likes to keep free; if you run him with a herd he makes a good loner. He's liable to pull something treacherous any time. You've got to watch this kind of nag."

Danny staggered as the man cuffed him a sharp glancing blow with the flat of his hand. "Just where do you come in on this deal, little friend?"

"Hey," Kristin said. "Let him alone. He's with me. Where's the ten dollars?" She flushed and bit her lip.

But the man stood over Danny. "You're a gypsy; where's your crowd staying?"

Danny held his fingers over his hurt but didn't flinch, gazing up with gentle black eyes. He was used to being nicknamed derisively; he'd always fought his way through his companions and by dint of wiry strength got accepted. Every new encounter to Danny meant the battle waged again. "My mother was, mister."

"Where's your old man? Is he here?"

"He's a farmer; he's not a gypsy."

"Where's your mother then?"

"She's dead." Danny stated it clearly, easily.

The man looked up and down the boy. "What'd you tell sweetheart here to do?"

"I know about the act is all, mister. From my mother. She used to tell me about horses and how the *gitanos* trained them."

Kristin patted the gelding, breathless, a little afraid. "Hurricane doesn't look treacherous to me, Danny. Can we go back and look at your horses, mister? You don't need to give me that money."

"Come on." He pawed in his pocket and brought out a huge leather wallet, extracted a bill. "Here."

The pair of children followed, Kristin leading the gelding. She looked at Danny who whispered, grinning, "You were good."

The man turned aside at a tent and spoke softly into the interior, but they heard: "Say, what you doing with a card game when the show's going on?" He withdrew his head and smiled at the two. "Got to keep these roughnecks on their toes." He breathed heavily, adjusting his round hat, "And I'm getting old."

He tied Hurricane alongside twenty-odd horses, ponies and mules, mostly ungroomed and scrubby, in the open roped stalls. The children walked in back of the animals and heard the names: Big Bess, Major, Silver, Babe, Ginger, Nip. One he called Blueberry, a little rough buckskin mare. "Don't know anyone wants one cheap, do you? Like to let this one go."

"What's wrong with the nag?" Danny shrugged, laughing.

"We don't need her and hay's too high for me. She's the foal of Ginger over there. She's not really broken yet."

"Don't you ride her?"

"When Ginger went lame we put her in the bear act for a couple of days. He rode her. I got too many of these brutes; they're all falling out of condition, too."

"How'd she work under the bear?" Danny asked.

"A little skittish. But I wish you'd have caught an act I had out East last year. A Norwegian stag that pulled a sulky cart. It was cute."

"What happened?"

"He smashed it up one day; vaulted clear into the stands. Broke his leg and we shot him."

"Wow," Danny said.

"How old?" Kristin spoke dreamily.

"Who?"

"This buckskin."

"She's just turned three. I'm going to get myself out of this business. And soon." He walked on further. "How you like this pair of broncs?"

Danny stayed half a step behind him. "Nice, Mister."

But Kristin's blue eyes were blazing like anger. She could not move from Blueberry's stall. She stood falling in love. The mare turned her head, the black mane drooped uncombed, the forelock straggled over her brown eyes; her slender almost-black legs contrasted with the sandy-colored coat. Field burrs had knotted in her tail. Like the others she needed grooming. They looked at each other and as the mare turned back to stand with head drooped, Kristin knew her desire.

Danny was coming back for her. "What's the matter?"

"How much does he want?"

"For the nag?"

"Yeah."

"Ask him, Kristin."

"You."

Danny called, "How much, mister?"

The man was returning. "Make me an offer."

"Fifty," Danny said.

"Seventy-five and she's yours."

"It's not for me, it's for her." Danny gestured to the staring girl.

"How long are you here for?" Kristin asked.

"Tomorrow night. But I can't hold her for you, sweetheart. I've told a couple of parties she's available. First one with the cash gets her."

Kristin flashed her smile upon him. "Hold her for me till tomorrow."

"Sorry."

"You've got to," she begged.

"No, sweetheart." He shook his head; his hand in his pocket jingled change.

Danny explained, "She's horse-nuts."

"They all are, that age."

"Why don't you give him the ten dollars to hold her?" Danny said.

"And if I don't come back tomorrow," Kristin cried, "you keep it."

"The two of you ought to go into business together. That's as fast a con job as I ever heard. It's a deal, sweetheart." Trumpets sounded from the ring. "That's my cue. Hang around long as you like. You're nice kids."

As he strode off, Kristin shouted after, "Can you have her delivered, please?"

The man halted and pulled off his derby, scratched his head. "I'm addled, I guess, but for seventy-five, all right!"

"He's over-charging," Danny whispered.

Kristin said, "If they don't let me have her, I'll do something."

Danny giggled. "When he first hit me I thought we were goners, didn't you?"

"I'll run away from home," Kristin declared.

"Turns out he's okay," Danny said. He pulled a broken piece of comb from his jeans pocket and ran it through his tight curls; he tucked his black jersey smoothly down in his pants. "I wouldn't mind to work here. I'd brush up these nags. Come on, let's look at the rest."

"I mean it, what I said. You go on. I want to stay here." She slipped into the stall beside the mare who soon was holding the button of Kristin's blue shirt in her teeth experimentally. "Danny," she called. "Is Blueberry the treacherous type?"

"Might be stubborn, but not mean," he shouted back. "She might balk on you till you straighten her out."

"I'll run away," she whispered.

And she repeated it to the family that night at the supper table. They'd laughed and dismissed the subject.

The buffet was spread in the dining room and the hired women tended the customers. Only for a real emergency would they bring a problem to Mother or Daddy.

"Don't be a baby," Mother patted Kristin's hand, the Persian curled on her lap.

And Daddy smiled. "I'll help you pack."

"Do you realize," Margo said, "that in three months I'll be gone to State, Astrid. You think you can handle everything? I don't want to let one of the animals go! I'll be back vacations."

"I know how you feel," Mother said. "And in another year you'll be going too, Astrid. It's going to be a problem. I don't see how you can keep the goats. I don't mind tending your smaller pets for you. I wish Kristin were more interested in the Nubians."

"I'm not going to college when I reach your age," Kristin told Margo. "I'm going to get a job and make money and no one can stop me then from getting my horse." The tears almost sounded in her voice and she speared a huge tomato chunk to stuff it in her mouth so they wouldn't notice. She spoke through it. "I'll take care of your dogs though, when you're both gone." She rested her sandals on Bimbo under the table, asleep.

"I thought about paying Danny Wasilewski," Margo said. "He lives nearby, and could do the cleaning out and carry the grain sacks, Astrid. You'd just have to milk and feed. I think he might do it for ten dollars a month. Should I ask him?"

"Think of someone else," Daddy said. "I don't want that gypsy kid around."

"Just during winters, Daddy," Margo said. "And he won't be playing with Kristin. I'll keep him busy."

"I've nothing against him personally," Daddy said. "But gypsies are a thieving lot, everyone knows."

"That's a lie." Kristin declared it, softly.

Daddy raised his eyebrows. "Manners, please. Keep such remarks in your own head. Once I saw one of their caravans at a fair. A man was talking to the crowd; he had a gold ring in one ear and a handkerchief around his head. We aim to give you an honest show, he said, but there are a few pickpockets around here so watch out for your pocketbooks, everyone. Well, each person put his hand straight on his billfold, and so the gypsies knew right where everyone's was."

Margo pushed back her hair, fluffing it, adult. "Oh, Daddy, really."

"Clever shoplifters, too. The women keep safety pins and hooks inside their jackets to lift the stuff."

Astrid protested, "Are you saying Danny steals?"

Kristin gazed at Margo. "Pay *me* that ten dollars every month!"

Margo paused. Astrid nodded, "Good idea. You know I have to get good grades in my senior year. I'll be real busy. I'd love it."

"Can you afford it, Margo?" Mother said, stroking her cat.

"No, but it's worth it," Margo said.

"I vote for it," Mother said.

Kristin stood up. "Listen. Please listen. Don't pay me the ten dollars, but give me all that hay the goats waste. I just threw more out on the floor this morning. I could feed a horse easy on that. And I'll tend the goats starting today. Astrid doesn't even have to come to the barn except to milk." Her intensity sparked through the room. She was grave and her voice quiet. "Daddy, I'm growing up. I'll be fifteen in spring. Everyone has got to stop treating me like they do."

"Everyone will," Daddy said, "when you earn it."

"I like the idea," Mother said. "I think it's mature of our Kristin to propose it. It'll mean a lot of work for her."

"It's ambitious," Daddy admitted. "But what does Kristin know about horses? She's only ridden at a stable a dozen times in her life. And horses are vicious sometimes. Don't they wear iron shoes and do dangerous things?"

"I won't have shoes on her, Daddy." Kristin was earnest. "She won't need them in the sand."

"Who is *she?*" Mother said.

"This Blueberry I was telling you about. I gave the man ten dollars to hold her for me until tomorrow. I was certain you'd let me buy her. She's so cheap. And she's young and I'll never need another horse!"

"I don't mind giving you the money," Daddy said. "I'm thinking of what the principle of the thing signifies."

"You always say that," Mother told him serenely. "I vote for Kristin and Blueberry. How do you stand, girls?"

"I vote yes," Margo said. "Lucky me!"

"Count me too," Astrid giggled.

"Before I exercise my right to stand and be counted," Daddy said, "tell us where you got the ten dollars, earnest money? I thought you had only the three I gave you for admission and sideshows."

"I won it."

"Ten dollars is a lot to win shooting tin rabbits like you did last year for that plaster doll!"

"In the rodeo," Kristin said. "Whoever could catch the bridle of the horse."

"Doesn't sound like much of a contest," Daddy said.

"Yes, but it's a trick horse and he let me. I entered the bucking contest too."

"You seem to have some special talent," Daddy said, "that I never noticed. I give in then. The vote's unanimous."

"Yeow," said Kristin, "Thanks, everyone."

Later, Daddy called the littlest out of the barn into the back yard. Benign, he had got the money from the till; he counted it into her grimy hand. Smoky was on the girl's shoulder, and she had a hayfork in her hand. Her braids glinted yellow in the last of the sun. Daddy shook his head. "I hope I'm doing the right thing. I wish I felt like the others about this. Are you sure you're big enough for this responsibility?"

"Daddy!" she frowned.

"And we have to have an understanding about your school work this fall and winter."

"Don't worry about a thing."

"Especially your math. I didn't like that *D*; it's a disgrace to you."

"I know!" She was ardent. "I'll study hard."

"And promises are made to be kept."

"Don't you worry." He watched her stride back into the barn.

III

Before the sun came up,

while it was yet dark, Kristin woke to the cardinal in the top of the tulip tree spinning a web of notes. Rain fell slowly, softly; the scent of the earth and grateful green things came through her window. She had a small room to herself at the head of the stairs; her sisters shared a big one down at the end of the hall. The bird, over its nest of bluish eggs, cinnamon speckled, cried to its soft-colored wife. Kristin got up and went to lean out the window, peering toward the barn and the tall tree; she couldn't see the bird. She slipped into her jeans and came down, softfooted. In the dining room she got a handful of paper-wrapped sugar loafs with a picture of a blue kettle on them. On the porch Bimbo's tail thumped; he remained on his side. The setters rose and paced after her as she ran down the path which was dusky now, predawn.

Daddy had put up posts and strung barbed wire across the end of the pasture fence where it was nailed to the barn. It made a paddock where the mare had been turned when she arrived late yesterday evening. She was used to no shelter and needed no more than the barn wall which was one side of her paddock.

Blueberry lifted her head as Kristin slipped between the sharp wire and stood with body tense, a leather goat-lead in one hand. The rain-washed yellowish-gray coat gleamed pale in the half-light; someone had cleaned the mare up a little and her mane wasn't so scrubby. She wore a little braided rope halter. She stood quietly gazing at Kristin who finally moved to approach and give her the sugar. The strong teeth crunched and the girl felt the slippery warm tongue. She stroked the silky face and the velvet skin about the lips. Making a slip-knot using the loop of the lead, she put it around the underjaw.

"Come on, girl."

The mare followed as she let down the four barbed strands which, fastened to a pole, made the gate. They went out to the road of gravel that led to the lake. She ordered the setters who were following to go home. She led the mare over to the ditch and stood her in it; she hiked herself up and swung a leg over. At a walk they started down the road; the air was coloring pink as the rays of the approaching sun raked up into the east sky. The rain was quitting. Kristin's knees pressed against the damp hide.

Kristin felt she had never known the kind of pleasure that welled up in her now; there was nothing quiet about it, but a wildness, new. "I wouldn't care if I died right now, Blueberry!"

The horse began to jog and, unsteadily, she shifted from side to side, grasping the wet mane hairs. "Ho," she whispered, and the mare shook her head, champing at the bit of leather around the jaw. The ears were pricked forward, watchful, and in a movement which Kristin came to recognize later, Blueberry gathered her muscles a little, ducked her head, and came down firmly on her two front legs, shying at some imagined terror.

Kristin was flung forward over the mane and onto the road, clinging still to the leather line. She gasped as she was jolted, but scrambled up at once. She felt a little betrayed as she led the mare to a ditch again and slipped up on her back. Her jeans, damp from the weather and the horse's soaked hide, were now muddy from the road. Her sneakers stuck to her feet.

Kristin knew that the strangeness of the route they were now taking would wear off in time, and also with practice she would learn to mount with less awkwardness. But she felt a piece of fear, realizing that her skill at riding was nothing and she had no saddle or bridle to give her superiority. All that held the mare to her was a slim leather line; if she broke loose, not yet knowing home and barn, the mare could canter for miles and be lost and gone.

She guided Blueberry by reaching down to turn her head this way or that; she kept the rein securely folded about a small strong hand. At the little sand path to the lake they turned off; Kristin kept the pressure of her legs even upon the flanks, speaking soothingly as they went, warily, over the bridge. The hoofs sank deep into the sand as they climbed the dune, mounting the steep side slant-wise, Kristin clinging to the mane to keep from sliding off, giving the mare her head. They jogged down the other side, and Kristin began to notice that Blueberry had two slow gaits: a trot which she sat with difficulty, and a comfortable single-foot in which the feet moved independently and smoothly.

At the foot of the blow as they were going at a quick clip, a rabbit sprang from the straggly grass under them. With a snort Blueberry slammed her forefeet down; Kristin was over her head, thudding into the soft sand. In an almost continuous movement the black forelegs went straight up to the sky over the prone body and balanced a moment. Then the horse wheeled and cantered back up the dune they had just come down.

Kristin, also continuing the movement of her body, was rolling to her knees and pulling herself to her feet, crying, "Ho, ho, Blueberry!"

She ran through the sand, up the hill, wondering in a detached kind of way who was making the moans, recognizing her own voice and unable to stop. "Oh, please, please, Blueberry. Come back."

But over the dune before the bridge to the road, the mare had halted to crop the grass edging the Wasilewski fenceline at its far boundary. When the girl came close, the animal snatched a mouthful and began to move down the path. "Ho." Kristin said it, low-voiced and firm. The horse waited, a wisp of green at its mouth, until she took the rein.

Kristin spent some time talking to her and feeding her handfuls of the grass. "Darling, darling."

She got on again and returned to where the mare had shied, urged her on when she hesitated, with heels and voice, and made her way to the sandhill overlooking the lake. There they paused for a time as Blueberry gazed at the meadow of water spread before. The sun moving softly behind them had circled all the horizon in lavender and pink, violet and peach. In the center of the rainbowing, the pair stood. The beach lay darkened yet in shadow, but the rays glinted over the lake, and the sandbars were pale streaks wavering not far from the shore. There was no wave movement and the whole world was at peace.

Kristin felt how, during this first ride, a new life was beginning; a thing that had been alive in a dream, so she had constantly to build it and give it dimension through deliberate story-telling which she managed to do in the tree-house, in her bed at night, or in the civics classroom or the study hall; this thing now had palpable proportions. That wildness, like daring, leaped in her again.

"Come on," she urged and the beast approached the lake with some wonderment. When her muscles gathered in the way Kristin had learned meant she wanted to shy, Kristin pressed with her sneakers upon her ribs, and the impulse went away as Blueberry was reassured.

They followed the shoreline north, meeting and seeing no one. Blueberry shook her head and Kristin clicked her tongue, and they cantered in a rocking-horse gait for two miles. A great bleached piece of driftwood, staggering out of the pebbly, packed sand at the water's edge, brought the mare to a standstill, but the girl was prepared and sat it out. They returned at the same easy gait and went home over the same way without incident. Along the last of the road, she let the mare walk to bring her in cool.

And then the skein of days went unwinding. There was in them a unique completeness, a fulfillment. When she turned to Blueberry in the blind instinctive way of one in first-love, yet unhurt, the mare was always there. Wherever possible Kristin moved with the horse at her side. Sometimes in the hot nights, noisy with the sounds of katydids and crickets, or a wakeful bird, she brought her pillow and quilt out to the paddock. The mare became so used to her presence that she wouldn't rise from where she rested, but watched the girl as she made her bed and lay down nearby. Kristin would awake to find the horse had risen and was chewing on her hay or waiting in soft silent animal fashion for Kristin to direct their day.

In her first week, the mare had kicked Kristin's thigh in a violent way when she had come up behind unexpectedly. After the first fright and pain the girl had found she was unable to keep her face from contorting. She realized there was no animosity in the blow, but she felt nonetheless as if a friend had turned upon her.

"I hate you," she had cried, on fire. "Darn you, anyway. You're such a dope. I wish I'd never got you. Hate."

And with an almost cruel movement she'd thrust the leather loop into the mare's mouth and jerked her head as she led her out. Easily, she leaped to her place on the warm back and they rode out at a fast canter. They explored the countryside. They waded streams. They followed the lake southward. The mare entered the creek which flowed to meet the lake. Snorting, she went in and then stopped midstream. She drank and then sighing with pleasure and grunting, sank to her haunches.

Kristin slipped off to stand in the shallow running water, canvas shoes and pants wet, and wait on her. There was none so darling! She rubbed the thigh-bruise; it was nothing at all!

If the late afternoon were hot, and she'd finished the barn work Margo set her, she got into her swim suit and they cantered down the long road to the water. The horse walked far out, until it was time to swim, Kristin staying on her back or holding to her mane, carried along. Blueberry grew fond of the water and its relief from the orb above that seethed like a cauldron and tipped the slow thick heat upon the blazing white sand.

Blueberry grew fearless and loped straight for the lake, plunging in, the foam like a wave surrounding and drenching them both. She would stand pawing the water, shaking her head, swimming out. When they emerged she rolled in the sand, falling to her knees with Kristin scrambling free. The mare stretched her neck, grinding the silica grains into her hide, blissful. Kristin encouraged her to roll over

and then, as the mare put out her forelegs to rise, the girl
would get on at the same moment. She had heard of trick
acts where you taught a horse to lie down that way on
command and to rise. She had seen pictures of horses kneeling for their riders or bowing to crowds. But Blueberry
wasn't that kind of horse and her mistress couldn't have
cared less.

She carried a cake of soap along one cool dawn as the
waves dashed about the rough lake. Kristin lathered the wet
hide and then led her into the surf again. As the suds
washed away, she slipped into her seat again and, chilled,
they tore up the sand hill and home.

She told Astrid her adventures. Her sister was in the
chicken house where a clutch of four enormous goose eggs
was hatching off. It was Astrid's first try at geese, the big
Toulouse breed that sometimes reached twenty-five pounds,
so the farmer claimed. They had been set under one of the
banty hens a month ago.

"Be still, baby," Astrid said. "I can hear them squeaking inside the shell. You're not supposed to help but I'm
dying of suspense."

"Don't touch them."

"I know." Astrid sighed, hovering above the shells,
some of which were cracking in dark thin lines, others of
which still sealed the birds in their oval world. "They'll
probably die anyway. I'll do something wrong."

Kristin left her. She took the pitchfork and went to
turn over the barn bedding. There was no fault to find
with the way she did her new chores. But sometimes, the
girl felt that in fall when Margo was not around with her
sharp eye and sarcastic tongue, she would feel easier. She
looked forward to winter. She confided in Astrid, "I'm

glad she's my sister, but sometimes I don't feel like we're any relation at all!"

Margo had found out about Danny being at the fair with Kristin, but hadn't told Daddy. It worried Kristin that she might use it some time when Kristin forgot or did something stupid. Margo was in the barnyard now with one of her boy friends. She wore bleached jeans and a white silk shirt. It was evening and they were watching the kids who came out every twilight to play wildly.

Margo had persuaded Daddy to make a low teeter-totter and the Nubians, especially the kids, loved the new toy. They walked with mock sobriety up it and let it balance and then tip down. All colors, spotted and speckled and solid-hued, they lined up sometimes, three or four or more, crowding each upon the other, their petal-like ears pricked forward past the tips of their noses. They waited to see what the plank under them would do.

The evening had turned cool and all the goats had walked out, relieved after the milking, satisfied with their feeding. The kids, irrepressible, snorted and in a covey were dashing madly about the yard. Ears flopping and flying, they went this way and that, this way and the other, ending with a scramble and a skidding halt at the teeter-totter.

Margo and her friend were talking; Kristin noticed their voices stop. She looked out the barn window to see the young man scrambling up on Blueberry's back while Margo held the rope halter. He started down the gravel road. Kristin darted into the yard.

"Hey! Come back!"

"He knows how to ride," Margo said. "I asked. He's a very good horseman. I couldn't say no."

Kristin threw down her fork. "Darn him. Nobody is supposed to ride my horse." She felt she was dangerous.

"You've got no right, Margo." She was shouting. "How dare you!"

"Keep your temper. What harm is it doing?"

She yelled, "You've got no right to let him get on my horse!"

"Stop acting like a baby, Kristin."

"Did you ever see a baby clean out a stable! I hate you."

Kristin dashed out to the road to see the fellow returning far down in the distance, Blueberry at a dead gallop. Kristin started jogging down the road to meet them, her anger a heavy pain, her jealousy almost weakening her. Then as they neared she saw that the mare was running away and she stopped, standing aside as they bolted by, the hoofs hammering dully, the dust rising behind.

Blueberry wheeled into the barnyard, the young man clutching the mane, nearly tipping off. Kristin ran after to watch as the mare skirted the teeter-totter, the Nubians fleeing, bounding, to the barn's shelter. The mare made a skidding standstill at the barbed wire of her paddock, her neck across the strands. She backed away as the barbs snagged upon her flesh, cutting it open.

The boy slid off and caught at the halter. He turned, apologetic, to Kristin streaking up. "She's cut herself," he cried.

Agonized, Kristin knew no anger, only fear. She examined the trickle of dark red. "It didn't touch the jugular. That's important."

"I don't think it's hit a vein at all, Kristin."

"The artery is what I'm worried about."

"She's okay."

"I don't know." Kristin watched how the blood following the fur in a dark line dropped slowly into the dust.

"I think she's all right."

"Do you?"

"I'll hold her if you want to put something on it."

"Okay. Be right back." She dashed to the house for water and soap and iodine.

It wasn't until an hour later while the mare was cropping at her hay, apparently undisturbed by the accident, that Kristin remembered. "Lockjaw." She was sitting on the stoop with the crow on her shoulder, gazing toward the paddock.

Astrid had three goslings in a pasteboard box; they nibbled, piping, at a mash she'd made of hardboiled egg and cornmeal. Astrid worried, "I don't think that other egg's going to hatch, but I left it with the hen anyway." She glanced up at Kristin who stood dramatic and pale. "What did you say?"

"Lockjaw. That's what she can get around barnyards from nails or something sharp, Danny said. That's why I watch the frog of her hoofs to see if there's a nail or anything."

"Come on, let's call the vet," Astrid said. And when she had talked over the phone she told Kristin at her side, "It'll cost ten dollars. He's coming right out to give her the shot."

"I don't care what it costs," Kristin vowed.

But Astrid told Margo and she insisted on paying. "It's only right, Kristin. He's my boy friend. I didn't know he made that up and never was on a horse before. I'll make him stick to his sports car. I'm sorry." She went away; they were going over to the movies in a nearby town.

Kristin paid no heed to her amends. "If something happens, I'll never forgive her, Astrid. I'll kill her."

"She's sorry," Astrid said. "Buck up."

"I'll run away from home, too." Kristin stood with Astrid in the yard before the horse. It was nearly dark and the sound of the mare munching hay mingled with an occasional chirrup from the chicken house where the fowl sought their roosts and jostled together as they settled, and with the baaing of two kids left in the yard and hoping someone would come to shoo them inside, and with the far-off horn of a locomotive announcing that it approached a crossroads.

The night was loneliness. Astrid went away to her room where Margo would come after a while. Then the moon, like a bonfire, was seen suddenly through the trees; it rose quickly and sat up high, white and quiet. Mother came out. "There isn't any danger now that she's had the antitoxin, dear."

"Maybe she'll have a reaction."

Mother held her big golden-eyed gray cat, stroking it while she looked upon the figure seated with legs drawn up leaning against the barn wall. "I doubt it."

Kristin shook her head. "What if I remembered too late?"

"Don't be silly; the vet said everything was fine."

"I never liked that vet. That time Babar broke his leg, he said he'd heal all right with a splint, and he didn't and we had to butcher him."

"That wasn't the vet's fault; a compound fracture is difficult to handle."

"What about him saying a shot would put that kitten to sleep when it got hurt! And it took an hour to die."

"Oh, Kristin, stop it now. That was three years ago. Come on to bed."

"I want to stay." She crossed her arms on her knees, resting her chin.

Mother sighed and left her there. At the porch Kris-

tin heard her speaking to Daddy. "After all, it's an experience."

"Fool kid!" Daddy exploded. "I never liked him hanging around our Margo."

"Margo's grown up."

"Eighteen isn't grown. I don't like her going off with
him to the movies tonight."

Their voices disappeared as they went in, the woman
reasoning and soft, the cat following her steps; the man
growling and protective, wanting his women close about
him, safe.

At midnight Kristin went in, stiff-muscled from the
cool ground and the half-napping she had done. She fell
upon her bed without taking off her clothes, slept rest-
lessly, dreaming violent unpleasant scenes that she forgot
when she woke at dawn. She went out to see the mare who
appeared as usual. For a week she worried around her,
watching for any unusual position or change in appetite,
anticipating disaster. Then gradually the terror faded and
made room for the happiness to return.

She rode the mare to the beach at night, riding beside
the pounding lake as the wind leaped fierce and warm, the
way it does before and after storms in unsettled summer
seasons. Kristin felt herself a part to the animal, how it was
winged, in the dark its legs not seen, in the noise of the
surf its hoofs not heard; so the two floated somewhere in
air.

Late in August one day she packed a lunch. Mother
was preparing a dish for the buffet table, seasoning ground
steak for the little meat balls. "You must expect to get
pretty hungry," she said as Kristin salted four cold boiled
eggs and put in rolls and jelly and peanut butter and a
dozen franks. "Put some of that back, dear, in the frig."

"No. I might stay till late, or eat two times. And one of the dogs might go with me too. I'm going to ride clear over to Bald Tom."

She put the food in a canvas sack with a few bottles of the root beer that the girls had made in a crock in June and capped when the yeast had worked well. She balanced the sack across Blueberry's withers and went off. Danny was waiting at the Wasilewski gate.

He had a worn-out leather line in one hand, eight feet long. "Look here, I'll show you something. You ought to have two lines when you ride so you can teach her to follow more signals."

He slipped off the long strap Kristin used to guide the horse. He laid the middle of the line he had brought in back of her ears. He led the ends along her cheeks and through her mouth from each side, running them back again, making two reins.

"That's an old gypsy way when you bring the *caballos* in from the field and they're not used to a bridle. Here's another one."

He took off the line and laid the middle this time in her mouth, knotting it underneath comfortably and putting a line end up on each side. Kristin took them from him. "I'll remember, Danny."

He sprang behind her onto the mare and they went double down to the shore. The day was bright and cool; they followed the lake north five miles and then turned up into the spare dune desert where Bald Tom reared, the highest point for over a hundred miles around. The face of the great sand hill was bare, the other three sides thickly wooded. The children dismounted and led the sweating mare as they climbed by devious paths or made their own way through openings in the trees and thickets.

Near the summit was a spring where they put the bottles in the sandy bottom and tied the mare up. They went above to sit at the head of the mountain of sand, looking out past the low dunes to the blue sweep that was Lake Michigan. The gold sun glinted and made the water a silk banner.

After a while Danny built a fire and they broke sticks to spear the franks. Danny went down for the root beer. "That's good stuff," she told him, "about five corks popped and it went all over the jam cellar. I had to clean it up."

"Where's the opener?"

She had forgot and there was no knife or other utensil either. Finally he pried the caps loose with rocks. They leaned against the tree boles; Blueberry dozed below, flies buzzed and stung. Danny said, "I might have to go away."

"Where!"

"To my Uncle Jock's. I never saw him in my life. He's my dad's brother."

"Why?"

"It's not settled yet. I said I wouldn't go. I ought to stay here. For one thing, my dad won't get along at all alone. But he says it's an opportunity because they'll pay me regular besides feed and board."

"That's awful."

"Well, it's not decided."

"Just say you refuse."

"That's what I'm trying to do, Kristin." The frown lines were furrowed on his young face. His dark eyes looked into the woods.

"How have things gone this summer?"

"We do pretty well with that vegetable stand. It's been a good enough year. The melons are coming in now.

But there's always some new kind of bug and we have to put cash out for sprays and everything. I don't know. I hate truck-farming. I like messing with horses."

"Me too." In a while she said, "Do you want to go to the Tri-County Fair with me?"

"When?"

"Day after tomorrow. I'm taking the bus."

"Are your sisters showing stock?"

"Yeah, and we can ride back with them. Margo won't tell. She's been nice lately ever since Blueberry got cut up on that barbed wire. It's an important show for them. They need blue ribbons if they want to sell the buck kids for any price at all."

"I know."

"I wish you'd come."

"I better not, Kristin. Look what happened last time. That guy socked me and then you got a horse out of it!"

"Yeah."

"And I have to work." Danny's mouth tightened and he looked older than his fourteen years. "I'm not going to Uncle Jock's. I'm sick of grubbing on a farm."

"Maybe he's got horses."

"I asked; there's not a nag on my uncle's place."

"Have some more peanut butter and jelly."

"If you get it out of the jar for me and spread it."

"Okay."

They were using a stick for a knife. "I'm lazy today!"

She got on her knees and loaded the last of the sticky stuff on the last roll and fed him while he lay back and opened his mouth and chewed and swallowed. They giggled as she tilted a bottle of root beer and some ran down his shirt. "Is it fizzy?"

"It tickles my ribs."

"You're crazy." She was delighted.

Then they buried the jam jars and bottles and clambered down the dune side, skidding and sliding. The trip took a fraction of the time it had taken to go up. Above, birds were asleep in branches; none moved or sang. In cool burrows rabbits sprawled side by side, snakes in a death-like doze coiled in the comfort of rocks and logs. The children rode double over the desert sand, sometimes chinking on an ancient arrowhead or spear point; no life was apparent although tracks of sand spiders and sometimes a toad or bird were seen. At the water they dismounted to wade, letting the sweat-darkened Blueberry trail after in the water, too. Halfway home, Kristin tired and Danny gave her a leg up. He walked beside. When finally they reached his farm she hesitated as he stood patting Blueberry's neck before he would turn in. She suddenly sensed an unexplained feeling like sadness.

"Don't go anywhere else to live, Danny. You're my best friend."

"I think I'll manage to stay. You're my best friend too, Kristin." He stroked the horse who nudged him with her nose. He ran his strong hand over the coarse shiny mane, and down the legs, lifting a hoof, examining it, his head bent, his face hid. "Remember to keep them cleaned out, Kristin. This frog needs some trimming; get your knife when you get home and do like I showed you."

"Okay," she whispered.

He turned, abrupt, sprinting toward the farmhouse, grayed and ramshackle. He waved back at the door before going inside, slamming it so it echoed out to where she sat on the mare.

❧ ❧ ❧ IV ❧ ❧ ❧

Kristin was alone in

the tall bleachers of the grandstand at the Tri-County Fair on Labor Day, while the man in the black top hat and breeches put the snow-white mare through an act billed as: *The World Famous Riding Master Monsieur Maxime, Pupil of the Royal Spanish Court, and His High School Mare, Silver Flame.* When he first cantered on, the horse knelt to the applause, and then it went through various tricks: walking sidewise, lying down, counting out answers, plucking a handkerchief from its master's pocket, and while he stood below flicking the whip, rearing and standing erect before him. Then music played a waltz as the mare danced in step and, pausing to bow again, cantered slowly away.

Kristin was dazzled. She wandered away from the crowded place to the barns where the stock were stalled and where her sisters were. She was to ride home with Margo who was going to pick up a display of her prize pansies which she'd been clucking over like a setting hen all summer long, hanging upon them so devotedly that Mother dubbed them *Margo's children.*

When Kristin reached her sisters Margo was furious. One of the best does, Queen, cream-colored and young, had developed a caked udder. "It's this darn drafty place they stick us in," Margo muttered.

53

Astrid was pinning an old red sweater on the doe, slipping the hind legs into the sleeves and buttoning it along the back, the milking sack protected by the wool. The fair would go on another day but Margo was taking the sick Queen home in the back of the Ford. Kristin helped lift out the seat and put in a tarpaulin and some straw. The doe pulled at the rope lead, her ears back in alarm; she panted a little. Kristin scratched her behind her ears and Queen leaned hungrily into her hand.

"I'm going to teach my mare tricks, Margo."

"Good for you."

"But I'm worried about how to start. Did you know that Blueberry used to do an act where a bear rode on her? A Wild Himalayan Bear! And I saw this white horse perform today."

"I think it's more than a draft made Queen ill. I think she's picked up something."

"It was a High School Horse act. First one I ever saw or heard of. Silver Flame, and the rider was from a Spanish king's court."

Margo stared ahead onto the white-hot highway before and listened to the heavy breathing of the fevered doe. "That's the best way there is to bring disease into a herd: showing at fairs!"

"Did you ever see that act, Margo?" Kristin gazed over at her sister's pretty, flushed face, the flaxen hair of her bun straggling softly about her ears.

"Did you ever hear that a veterinary keeps disease in his shoes, going from place to place? Fair exhibitors too."

Kristin shrugged. "I was telling you about this horse act. Don't you listen?"

"Sure." Margo drove a little fast, but she'd never had an accident. She rounded a bend so the doe staggered.

"Watch out," Kristin told her.

"I'm late. But I'll slow down." Half angry at losing a potential first ribbon on Queen, she glanced at the littlest. "There won't be time for me to mess around with her. I've got to get my pansies together. Could you put the hot packs on Queen?"

"I wanted to ride. Blueberry hasn't had any attention all day. Why can't you?"

"Time, obviously. I have to save *time*."

The two girls had tempers almost equal, and neither had Astrid's placidity or humor which was like their mother's. Kristin felt a familiar stubbornness that had nothing to do with rationality. "What's time? The Nubian judging's over and the pansies aren't till tomorrow. So you can get back as late as you like. Astrid won't care."

"I've got a date. He's coming to the barns to pick me up. And I don't know where he's staying so I can't let him know if I'm going to be late."

"Daddy said you shouldn't go out with strangers."

"Are you going to tell?"

"I might."

"I wish you would, Kristin. That'd be fine." Margo's voice was hot and high. "I wish I hadn't voted on you getting your horse. And I heard Daddy say he wished you didn't have her too. I hope he makes you sell Blueberry."

"You shut up." Kristin's eyes were violet.

"How are you going to take care of her and do the barn work this winter too? The work is a lot heavier when the stock have to stay in most of the time."

"I can do it."

"And when I think of your studies!"

"Shut your mouth." Kristin gazed at the road, the tears flooding her eyes.

"You got a *D* in math last semester, and you're so dumb you'll never bring it up. You'll have to sell Blueberry. And I won't vote any more on your side."

Kristin felt the burning water on her cheeks. "Pipe down," she whispered, hoarse, at the eldest.

"So you better take care of this sick doe, Kristin."

"Okay," Kristin blurted, yelling, "now are you satisfied?"

They remained in their angry silence, Kristin leaning to the animal and whispering to it, petting it; her sister was speeding, an eye on the rear-view mirror for cops. They dashed up Highway 12; customers' cars were crowded in front of the restaurant; Margo drove around in back and braked.

Kristin got out stiffly, and while Margo ran around the buildings to where the flowers were bedded, she urged the creamy Nubian doe, constricted by the woolen covering, to climb out. She led her toward the milking room where she'd bring the pail of hot Epsom-salt-water and the ragged towels put aside for that purpose. She heard Margo's angry call:

"Kristin! Come here."

"Wait till I put this goat away, darn it," she yelled back. She dragged at Queen's collar, "Come on, come on, girl." Pushing her into the barn, she closed the door and ran, glancing at Blueberry as she passed the paddock, afraid the mare had done some wrong.

Margo was leaning over her trampled plants, crooning. The dark red and lavender faces, yellow and blue, specked and dotted, were broken-stemmed, ravished. "Kristin. *She* did it. I've been nursing these pansies along for two years; they're from seed!"

Kristin stood terror-struck. "She couldn't; she's in her lot."

"They were my special babies. They were my babies!"

"Kristin!" Daddy was shouting from the back porch.

"It wasn't Blueberry, Margo," she said firmly and ran; she paused and looked up at the man on the stoop above her.

"Is Margo crying?" he said.

"I don't think so. I don't know. What else did she do?"

"She got in with the goats by the time I found her." Mother's singing came out from the kitchen and her calling to one of the hired women. Daddy shook his head. "How are you ever going to make it up to Margo?"

Kristin felt the hard thing in her throat and shrugged. "I don't know."

"You better start thinking about it before we meet at supper tonight."

She said, dry-throated. "Margo has to go back to the fair. They're staying late tonight."

"Is she meeting some boy there? I want to know."

"No, Daddy. She and Astrid are going to see the grandstand show. They've got some kind of horse act or something. Monsieur Maxime." She felt somehow that it was the children against the parents, leagued. "How did Blueberry get out?"

"She worked her latch loose. She ought to have a real gate, not that makeshift one I rigged up. And she trampled her way into the pasture where the fence is low. We simply don't have the time or money for a horse on the place. I don't mind your sisters' goats because theirs is a project that's bringing in money, and Margo's salary justifies extra expenses."

"But I'm paying by working for Margo." She felt her minority position.

"The mare got cut up a little where she broke into the pasture." He stopped her as she abruptly turned away. "It's nothing; Mother even had the vet come and look."

"Oh boy! Thanks."

"Don't thank me, Kristin. I'm fed up with the whole project of your horse. I talked to Mother about it. You aren't fifteen yet."

"Daddy!"

"I say we ought to get rid of her at this time. I'm going to be firm, Kristin."

But she ran away from him, shaking her head, to the buckskin mare. She threw her arms about her. "If they send you away, I'll go too." She and the horse against the world, she thought, and closed her eyes, feeling the rough new scars along the neck where the scratches were; and there were the old hairless lines where the skin was ripped earlier in the summer so the coat would never again lie perfectly smooth. The horse stood quiet under her embrace; she felt the throbbing of the pulse, the sighing of the breath. She heard Margo come up behind her.

Her sister seemed almost cheerful. "I'm not mad, Kristin. The heck with the pansies." Margo was pale. "And I don't think an animal ought to be responsible for what it does. A horse ranks lower than dogs and cats as far as IQ's go too."

Kristin looked at her. "Thanks for saying that. But you were telling the truth. Daddy's mad and he says I can't keep her."

"Because she broke out?"

"And because I don't have any money."

"That's silly. I'll talk to him."

"Really?"

Margo shrugged, attempting a smile. "I can get Mother on our side too."

"And Daddy said do you have a date, and I said you and Astrid were going by yourselves to the grandstand."

Margo laughed. "I didn't mean to be so stinky before."

"I won't get mad at you again, Margo." Kristin vowed it, felt her heavy debt.

She hurried to the milking room, and for an hour worked on Queen, applying the packs, reheating the water on the little hot plate that stood on a low shelf above the cement floor. She heard the car when it started up and Margo drove away. She wondered how the argument had gone. She turned the doe into a little stall, fed her and then went past the mare to the pansy bed.

Glancing about to see that she was alone, almost embarrassed, she raked and smoothed the earth, gathered together the ruined stuff and salvaged the plants still rooted, and with green leaves and some unbashed flowers. She brought a sprinkling can of water; then she went to examine Blueberry's latch. She hunted out a chain from the barrel of odds and ends in the garage and wired a swivel-snap to it, fastening it to the paddock's makeshift gate as an extra precaution. She went to the house and Mother called from the kitchen.

"Kristin, dear."

"What."

"Daddy's pretty upset. But I think it's all right, and you can keep her." Mother was on a stool, stirring a bowl that rested on her white-aproned lap.

"Oh, Mother."

"You've got Margo to thank." Mother had always seemed girlish and young. Suddenly Kristin saw how the smile-lines about her eyes and mouth-corners were engraved, and two frown marks were puckered between the brows. Mother spoke, almost severe. "You're big enough to know that things aren't going well this season. Naturally Daddy's worried. We haven't had such a poor summer for a long time. There are too many new places starting up along the highway and people want to try them out even if they're our steady customers. And with Margo off to college this fall, Daddy has a lot of troubles."

"Mother, I'll do anything."

"I know you will, dear. You've got more than enough enthusiasm. I'm just asking that you think things out ahead of time. There's no excuse for your horse breaking out; you ought to have known her latch wouldn't hold. That's not Daddy's affair, nor your sisters'."

"I know it!"

"Just *think*, Kristin."

"I will!"

"And you're going to have to get good grades, you know. I must side with Daddy if it's a question of schooling."

"I *will*." She stood like a small viking, straight and dedicated, her long braids down her back, her fingers puckered from the hot water, her face dirt-streaked, heated.

Mother smiled, shaking her head. "Will you ever grow up?"

"I am."

"Your sisters weren't a bit like you; they were tidy. You're such a tomboy, dear."

Kristin looked at her hands. "They're clean."

"But your face."

The mirror was on the back of the door where Mother kept herself pretty with lipstick and comb. Kristin hated her image. "Ugh."

"Margo wears gloves in the garden and the barn. You know she does, and uses nail polish and just gallons of hand lotion every year. Why don't you practice acting like her for fun now and then?"

"If only I were a boy."

"Have you thought ahead to how you're going to winter your mare?"

"What do you mean!"

"I've been waiting for you to bring it up. Because Daddy's bound to pretty soon. And you mustn't expect him to help you. Blueberry doesn't have any sort of shelter and it's the first of September."

"I *have* been thinking about it, Mother. Danny's going to help. We'll use some old lumber off his place." She felt Mother's wise eyes upon her as she garbled her words and made it up. It was true: she hadn't given a stable any thought; she was everything they said she was. She sighed.

Then in the morning, on the school bus, she looked around for Danny. She hadn't seen him since the trip to Bald Tom. She had ribbons tied to her braids, a desperate gesture toward the femininity her mother desired in her; they matched her dress. But Danny wasn't on the bus; she remembered what he'd said about his Uncle Jock, and felt sure that he was gone from the Wasilewski farm. She managed to get through the sessions in the classrooms where books were assigned and former classmates greeted.

When the bus jolted back over the narrow black macadam byroad, and dropped her off at the *Blue Coffee Kettle* that night, she dashed to her room and changed to her jeans. She was off on Blueberry, cantering down the woods path to the Wasilewski place. She ran up the porch and Danny's dad, looking harassed and busy, opened the door.

"Go look in the field, Kristin. He's busy with the cabbages. He's not going to go to school."

"You *have* to send him to school, Mr. Wasilewski!" Blueberry nickered from where she stood tied at the tree. Danny was coming; he waved.

"He'll go next week," the man offered, hesitant. "Another school."

She ran to meet Danny. "I thought something had happened."

He shrugged. "It *has* in a way. I leave next Tuesday."

"Five days. You can't."

"It's not so bad. And I'll be back next summer, maybe."

"You won't. You won't come back."

He was firm. "I will." He spit at a stone in the grass, hitting it. He hitched at his belt, a homemade leather one, his jeans low on his hips.

"I've got a problem." She told him about the need for shelter for the mare.

"I thought your sisters'd let you have a piece of their barn."

"No. You don't know my family. They're always saying, 'Is Kristin *ever really* going to grow up?' That's why they never remind me of anything. And it's true; I *am* a dope; I never thought about a stable."

"What'll your old man say if I come around to help you, Kristin?"

"He just said till school started. And you can stay back out of sight!"

They almost whispered it together, allied. Danny

leaned over the road and with a stick made sketches in the dust. "We'll use the barn side for one wall. And we'll make it a box stall so you don't have to tie her up. And we'll build it high enough to cut a hole through to the loft of the goat barn in case you ever buy some hay special for her, and want to push it through into her manger."

"Say. Nice."

"That's about it. We'll tear up one of those sheds down in the orchard. There ought to be plenty of good planks. We'll need a crowbar and hammer."

"I wanted to tell you about a High School act I saw at the Tri-County Fair last week. Monsieur Maxime from the Spanish king's court. Silver Flame!"

"Go on."

They spoke, intense, as if the rest of their lives stretched endless together, as if the coming days were a year.

On Saturday, as soon as she could get away, Kristin met Danny. They began assembling lumber, taking apart one of the tumbling buildings, salvaging the wood least rotted. They saved nails in a rusty bread tin that turned up. They made a rigging of branches, Indian style, and Blueberry dragged it through the woods path to the edge of the goat pasture, Kristin at her halter, Danny in the rear. The wind, presaging fall, whimpered through the changing leaves, damp and chill. While they went back and forth and when they rested, letting the mare crop grass, Danny talked to Kristin about schooling her horse.

"But how do I know she can learn?" Kristin said.

"Any horse that knows enough to eat hay when he's hungry can learn tricks."

"I thought there were secrets. I read that a lion-tamer has to be naked the first time he goes in the cage so they know his special scent. And they dope bears and tigers or hypnotize them at first. And the trainers can't work if anyone watches." She appealed to him; their eyes were on a level, hers blue, his so deep they were almost black.

"Bosh, my mother said." He dismissed it. "But you have to listen to me, Kristin, and get it straight. Maybe you ought to bring your school notebook and I'll write down some things. In certain ways you *are* dumb, Kristin."

"I'll bring it down to the woods after supper."

"That act you saw wasn't truly High School; it was a trick act. Real High Schooling's hard; that's *haute école* and they've been using it for centuries, especially in Europe. In Vienna they've got the Imperial Spanish Riding School. You can teach Blueberry a few High School gaits like walking sidewise or waltzing if you want. I'll show you. Takes time."

"Hey."

"First I want to give you whatever tack I have, Kristin."

"And that crazy sidesaddle!"

"It's yours. And there are a few lines and rope you can have. See, first you have to throw your mare on her side."

"I don't want her hurt."

"Come on, this is the last load. We'll start building tomorrow. You better tell your father I'm helping. Tell him I'm going away and he won't be mad."

She would not answer. She took the mare's head and they went down through the woods.

That evening Kristin had her notebook as she went riding through the woods, Smoky on her shoulder, the long lace dangling from his leg and looped around her wrist. When the horse's gait unsteadied the crow, he rode with wings half spread, open-beaked, crouching. At a steep almost vertical hillside above a ravine, she dismounted and descended, leading Blueberry. At the creek at the bottom, she went over a bridging fallen tree, leading the mare who stopped to drink and then padded across, leaped up the bank like a dog and followed Kristin, head at her heels, as she wound through the trees.

Danny was waiting. There was a sheltered spot above the creek where the children had once played pirates, using the spreading roots of an upturned oak for a ship. There they had dug out the bank and made a cave, shoring it up with saplings and binding them together overhead. Now he was leaning back in the mouth of the cave as if asleep. He opened his eyes.

"Halt and give the password."

"Silver Flame."

"Pass through the lines."

She put Smoky down and the crow wandered about plucking at insects and croaking in short gasps. They watched him; when the last of the sun came wavering through the trees' leaves catching his feathers, they lit up, irridescent. He preened a wing with his sharp yellow beak. "Crazy," Kristin said, tender.

She flung herself down by Danny. The mare stood over them, hipshot, while the boy talked. He had brought some ropes and straps along and had been rubbing some oil into the old leather. He stopped explaining after a while and got up, and while Kristin sat back and watched, he worked over the mare in the clearing before the cave. The ground was soft and mulched from the leaves that fell and remained.

Danny fastened a wide leather band about the mare's belly, behind her front legs. About her left fore pastern he put a little strap and lifting her foot, buckled it to the band, so she stood on three legs, one immobilized.

He took hold of her little rope halter, standing at her

right shoulder. He turned her head toward him and leaned against her so she fell upon her left knee, grunting a little. She put her teeth against her knee joint and nibbled at it. Danny began to push at her shoulder. Alarmed she made a violent movement to rise, and the pressure on the strap about her leg was so great it broke the leather, corrugated with age. She stood on all fours again, quiet.

"Too bad," Danny said. "One thing about horses, they don't forget. That's why you can start a lesson one day and take it up where you left off a week later. Now she thinks breaking the strap's what she's supposed to do. Let me see the rest of that stuff."

He went through the straps, found a more durable one, fortified it with rope and made another rig for the left leg. This time, after she had got to her knee and Danny pushed to make her turn on her side, she made the same rising movement. But the straps held; worried, she continued the upward gesture until she stood rearing, pawing out with the free leg. He waited on her, gentle, as she struggled with the held foot and then landed heavily on her free right foreleg.

The mare's eye went whitely over to Kristin as if she were hunted. Unlike the humans, or Bimbo, or Mother's cat, Mr. Shams, Blueberry didn't have binocular vision; her eyes were set on the sides of her head like those of the rabbits or the Nubians or of deer; this gave her a perfect field of vision for detecting pursuers. But her eyesight now was limited to one eye, and Danny and Kristin's figures were vague to the mare, and a little threatening.

Kristin saw the emotion and flushed. "What's the matter with her!"

Danny looked at the girl winding one of her braids about her wrist; the crow had come to her shoulder and watched with bead eyes. "If you're getting mad," Danny said, "you might as well give up horses. She won't hurt herself if you don't rush her. Try and think the same as she does. She has no idea what's in your mind, Kristin."

"She's scared."

"My mother said if a horse was afraid of something, and then some human whipped him past it, the horse would think whatever he shied at was what hurt him. He doesn't understand the whip. And his eyes are different than ours." The boy was fastening another rope about her front hoof that stood on the ground. He slipped the end of the rope through the belly band. "Try to get into Blueberry's mind."

"Yeah."

This time when Blueberry went on one knee he pulled on the rope, forcing her upon her two knees, kneeling, putting her nose against the ground in a half-surprised way. As the boy pushed her shoulder, she began to give little moaning sighs, half-grunts the way she'd done the time Kristin rode her into the creek where it met the lake, and Blueberry had sat on her haunches, dog-like. Her noises were almost contented; her mouth was turned aside so far it pressed Danny's jeans. With a final grunt as Danny gave her a push, Blueberry fell on her side with a soft thud.

"Now she won't ever mind lying down again, Kristin. As long as you're careful."

He was kneeling, removing the straps; the mare lay almost unnaturally docile, half-closing her eyes, as the boy stretched her legs out, rubbing them, talking to her, "Hey, hey, girl." He seated himself on one haunch and Kristin began to giggle. When Blueberry tried to raise her head, Danny pulled it back gently and she lay still, the boy's hands caressing her head.

"She's helpless, Danny."

"That's the idea. It does something to her mind knowing that she's under your control. And it doesn't hurt her spirit."

Kristin was almost maternal, fervent. "I wouldn't let you do it if it did. I don't want any part of her broken. I want her happy."

"From this point you can teach her to sit and to kneel easily. Now for some other tricks, get the notebook."

She sat on the ground at the horse's back, using the prone warm body to lean upon, and Danny wrote out instructions. Then he let the mare up and put the strap on the left foot again. When she went on her knee, he lifted the right foot and bent it so she was kneeling. With willing groans, as he leaned, she went onto her side.

Kristin was entranced. "I'm not going to tell anybody. It's going to be a secret until I've got her all trained."

"That's the last I'm going to have to do with her, Kristin. She's your mare. Now you go ahead and lay her down."

"Take Smoky."

"Okay."

"Come on, Blueberry."

She loosened the strap and urged the mare to rise. Blueberry lurched to her feet. Then with hands like a lover's, Kristin took up the dusty black hoof which she kept polished with linseed oil, and strapped it up. She pulled the mare's head, the long dark mane and forelock sleek from grooming, toward her and leaned. Blueberry knelt slowly and drew her other foreleg under her too. As if spellbound, as Kristin pushed, she slowly lay over, flat.

All the way home Kristin talked about it. Danny left her at the edge of the wood. She turned the mare into the paddock and went into the house. She spoke to Daddy, brave. He was in a big rumpled easy chair with a book. He looked up absently.

"Danny's going away to live at his Uncle Jock's."

"Who?"

"Up in Northern Michigan. Two hundred miles. And I have to have a shelter for my horse, too."

"I wondered whether you'd ever think of that," Daddy said, eyebrows up, quizzical.

"Can Danny help me on it? Tomorrow's Sunday and he can do it in a day. He'll help me clean out the buck house first."

Mother spoke up from across the room, her book on her lap propped against her cat. "Why is Danny going? Don't they live alone there?"

"Isn't there a Mrs. Wasilewski?" Daddy said.

"And I think it's awful people have to be so poor!" The littlest faced her parents, outraged. "Everybody looks down on them and the only reason Danny has to go away is because of money! If I had any money of my own, I'd give it to the Wasilewskis!"

"Well, *this* family hasn't been doing too well in that department, Kristin," Daddy said, tolerant. "And how do you propose to finance this affair? I didn't mind buying the horse, though I was against it. But a stable, with lumber high, is going to cost near as much as the horse."

"I'm getting it from Danny's farm." She was triumphant. "And it doesn't cost anyone a cent."

"Then you've *seen* him?" Daddy asked, "Against my wishes?"

"Only since school started. You said till then." She pleaded, "Can he help me!"

"All right." He ducked his head into his book. "Now stop bothering us."

"Thanks, Daddy." She blew Mother a kiss. "Goodnight!"

As she sped away she heard Mother, persuasive, "She's

showing initiative for the first time, dear. Hand me that brush; his tail is all knotty."

"You call that initiative? When someone gives her the lumber and does the work for her?"

"Danny's bright," Mother coaxed. "That's the trouble with long-haired cats. Why were you born a Persian, Mr. Shams?"

And Daddy was muttering; Kristin knew it was, "Gypsies. Poles."

She rejoiced. It took a legitimate *gitano* to know how to school a trick horse. What if Danny's mother hadn't been a true one and born in a carnival! Kristin hated to think of it. She praised her luck stars. She counted the steps up, reciting a jump-rope song:

> *Hi, Marshall Dillon,*
> *How about a date?*
> *Meet me at the corner*
> *At half past eight!*
> *Bring your horse,*
> *Bring your mule,*
> *Don't bring the teacher*
> *Because I hate school!*

Her voice rose higher and higher, shrieking the last. Her sisters shouted from their room at her.

"Pipe down, baby!"

"Be still, Kristin, we're talking!"

She called back at them, "Why did the cellar stair? Did it see the kitchen sink?" And slammed her room door after her.

She went and stood at the window, thinking how she had never been so content. Lucky me with Blueberry, and Danny to help me on the stable! But down inside the sick thing turned over and over, the thing that talking and laughing and singing and dancing, nothing could change: Danny was going away.

After a while she was able to go to bed. She could hear muffled noises from the barns, a baaing now and then, the squeal of Margo's banty rooster, and sometimes a whinny. She remembered that morning just a few weeks ago when she'd come down to ride her own mare for the first time. Sighing, counting over how blessed she was, she went to bed to lie half-awake for hours, restive as the thing inside turned and worried at her.

Then in the morning all she could do was laugh because Danny had cut holes in his straw hat and set it on Blueberry's silly head. The mare followed their movements about the yard, waiting for them, her meal over. They cleaned the dairy down with a hose, and then went to the buck quarters, pitching the odorous used straw out, and with a shovel, scraping the cement floor clean, sprinkling white lime, and scattering fresh bedding. The bucks, two old ones and a newly-purchased buckling, brown and white and tan mottled, came to watch, gravely, sometimes coming inside, hoping to be shooed out. They trotted away when Kristin shouted, "Scat!" The new one snorted and gamboled in the brisk air; he was silken with a white blaze on his face, his nose-ridge high and elegant, his jaw almost undershot. He shook his head gaily, bleated and ran stiff-legged.

"You're not going to have much time for working with Blueberry," Danny said, "with all this work, Kristin." He was cutting the wires that held the bale of straw together, and was spreading it.

She shrugged. "And I have to get good grades, too. I'm glad you said horses can remember!"

He'd hung his denim jacket on a post of Blueberry's lot. The goats came up and nibbled the zipper, and then chewed the frayed edges of the sleeve-cuffs. Sensing their naughtiness, some of them scurried off as Kristin and Danny came up; others stood their ground. They felt the autumn in the air, knew the male goats were nearby, and sometimes fell to butting heads together in long rhythmic half-playful half-incensed battles, until their polls were red and sore, and Astrid would have to separate them until the game was forgotten.

"Keep that pan of nails away from the goats," she told Kristin. "They'll knock it over." As she spoke a yearling upset the bread pan. They went to put their noses almost under Danny's hammer, curious, their flopping ears in the way.

"It's hard to work around them, Astrid," Danny said, as Kristin knelt and began hunting and picking up nails, "but don't run them off. I like them."

"So do I," Kristin said.

When Danny began the work on the stable, Blueberry was let free to roam among the Nubians. She got on well with the animals; she sneaked away and into the barn, and the does stayed about her, quiet. Astrid decided not to worry since she wore no shoes of iron and if startled, could do little damage.

Margo might have objected, but she was busy at packing to leave for Michigan State College in a couple of days. Margo was keeping Bimbo beside her, and she fussed over her banties a little, too. She was willing to turn the goats over completely to the competent Astrid, and to trust that Astrid would supervise little Kristin properly, now and through the winter.

Danny worked, the lumber scattered about the paddock. He'd put the struts in. Having the barn wall for one side of the shelter made it simple to build. He drove no posts, but fixed the planks to the side of the barn with long spikes. He decided against the loft-hole. "I'd like to put one in for you, but we don't have much lumber that's good, Kristin, and besides we're short on time."

"That's all right. I won't be buying hay anyway." She was his slave, adoring. "Can I get you a peanut butter and jelly sandwich?"

"Yeah."

Astrid was grooming her setters, combing the feathers along the backs of their forelegs. They stood immobilized with pleasure, nudging her when she turned from one to the other. She looked at the boy and girl. "Why do you children eat that stuff? Get him some apples or a chicken leg, Kristin."

"I'd as soon have what she said," Danny told Astrid, shy. "Do you have two kinds of jelly, Kristin? Got any strawberry jam? If you have, make me one of everything!"

Capable, he whacked the nails; he even swung on a door with a rusty large old-fashioned pair of hinges he'd taken off a broken-down one and oiled up a little. They still squeaked. Kristin brought the sandwiches, handing them up to him on the roof where he nailed shingles. She had a paper cup of milk, too. "Here."

"There won't be a window," he said.

"Who cares? Cut the door in half. Make it a Dutch door!"

"Okay. But I need another set of hinges. You run back and see if you can find one. Take this screwdriver, but you'll need a crowbar too. I think I stuck it up in one of those apple trees!"

"Hey!" she yelled, and dashed for Blueberry, who was

chewing hay from the barn floor, the straw hat still on, searching out the green stems, working her lips like an elephant's trunk, pliable, selective. Kristin led her out and leaped on her bare back. They charged down the woods path where they had gone once so carefully. Blueberry knew the way. The hat flew off and Kristin felt the beat of the hoofs under her, the swell of love for the beast that was the other part of her.

She swung off and dropped the lines, and while Blueberry hunted apples in the grass, digging into them with sharp teeth, slavering so her mouth sides and the leather line on her tongue, foamed, Kristin labored about, turning over boards cast aside, finally locating a bent pair of hinges. She got them off with difficulty with the crowbar, pinching her hand, bruising it and drawing some blood. She ignored the hurt.

They raced back, pausing long enough to replace the straw hat on the mare's ears. At an easy single-foot they ambled through the yard, to the boy. He had finished to the point of bedding the stall down with straw. "Astrid says you'll have to buy your own after this," Danny told her. "This is her housewarming present."

"Okay."

"Why don't you ever think of the future," Danny asked. "Like how you're going to manage *that* problem, Kristin?"

"I will! Not now."

And they went down into the woods to the secret spot where they'd been the night before. Danny sprawled near the cave. "I'm tired. I've been doing the work. I'll watch you."

The horse knelt but refused to go down. Kristin was patient and on the third try Blueberry sighed and curled her legs and settled onto her side. "The darling! Look at her, Danny."

"I've got to go home, Kristin. I've been away all day, and I have to talk with my dad. I don't know how he's going to get along. He won't ever start work if I'm not around to suggest what we do next."

"I'll drop in and visit him when I can." Her body had stiffened; she turned to Danny, pain-shot.

"All right, Kristin." His face was thinner-appearing in the early twilight. "And I think we might as well say good-bye here and now."

"That's a good idea." She spoke, bold. "Write me if you feel like it." She pulled at the mare's leg strap, bending over, unfastening it, letting the animal rise.

"I'm not much of a writer, Kristin."

"Drop a card if you get a chance."

"You too. I'll send you my address. And I'm *Daniel Wasilewski*. Don't write *Danny*."

"Okay."

He shook her hand rather formally and stroked the mare. He cleared his throat. "And remember," he said, "to think as Blueberry thinks. It's not hard, and you have a knack. And don't hurry her. She's got a little tendency to get balky and that's when you have to keep your temper. Okay?"

"Yeah."

"Keep her bending to the rein, so her neck curves pretty; don't let her stargaze."

"I know."

He sighed. "My mother used to be as horse-crazy as you are. She read to me out of the Bible where it says, *And I saw Heaven opened, and behold a white horse; and he that*

sat upon him was called Faithful and True. She didn't go to any special church, but she was what I call religious."

"Yeah, Danny."

"She used to say, if you do good you'll feel good, and if you do bad you'll feel bad. They can't teach you any better than that anywhere." The boy sounded angry.

"She made me a deck of cards, with the *gitana* queen, and the *crayí,* and a horse-trader for the jack with a cap made from a square of cloth knotted at the corners. You can't tell one back from another, and you'd never know they were handmade."

"Take them along to your uncle's."

"She carved me a set of dominoes too, once."

"I'd like to see your cards, Danny."

"I wish my mother were alive now."

"Me too."

"I'm always dreaming about her. Do you think that's her coming to visit me? Or is she really gone forever."

"Who knows, Danny?"

"When my father was out of his head after she died, he told me she'd promised to come overhead every noon time, and if he had something to say she'd hear him."

"Do you believe that?"

"No." He stood patting the dun mare. "In a way I hate to leave her. She's not bad, you know, for your first horse; you could do a lot worse."

He walked off into the woods as the early night darkened. A cuckoo far away played its tune to itself; else, all was still.

V

"She sure needs grooming,"

Astrid said to Kristin.

"I can't help it."

Astrid's hands were full; she was feeding birds and had a half grapefruit rind of suet melted into bread crumbs and chopped peanuts; she had some string to tie it from a branch. There were a couple of mesh bags too, with an apple and a lump of the stuff she concocted out of cornmeal and hot lard and peanut butter and poured into paper cupcake molds; the birds were crazy about Astrid's mixes.

The girls were looking into the stall through the top of the Dutch door in the November wind; the hinges creaked. "I've got to clean out the guinea pig house first, Astrid."

"Too bad."

Blueberry was lying down, nuzzling hay in her manger box; she laid in a position so her foreleg and flanks were soiled and caked. Her winter coat was growing in wooly underneath, and she looked rough.

"Ugh," Kristin said.

"Take time out and work on her for fifteen minutes." Her sister egged her on. "Where's your curry comb and brush?"

"No." Kristin, a tin bushel-basket by its rope handle in one hand and a sawed-off spade in the other, hurried off.

It was a Saturday; the short spurt of Indian summer was done. The leaves in the yard and woods fell from the shocked trees, sometimes overnight; a golden tree or one multi-hued, would appear changed in a cold clear morning, up to its knees in leaves, naked, black branches etched on a crystal sky. The air was clean, and leaves and twigs far away seemed telescoped and at hand; outlines and edges were plainer than usual.

The cavies were hardy and lived all year round in a dog house, tightly-made and once green-painted with a shingled roof, the back hinged for easy cleaning, the sign just legible over the front door: *Beware Of The Tiger*; he'd been Bimbo's predecessor, a cocker spaniel. The five pigs squeaked, hearing Kristin's approach. When she removed the back they scuttled, still shrieking; the long-haired male jiggled his hind feet, his pink eyes on Kristin. Teddy was soiled and needed his matted fur unknotted. She ought to take fifteen minutes for him also, set him on her lap and comb him until he was soft and silky again. Or else she ought to sell him and buy a short-haired male, ordinary, like the others. Kristin felt harried.

She'd had the female cavies for a few years; they were tame and knew her hand. She was curious always about the young they would beget, running about like miniature adults one morning, arriving when they pleased, their number and colors unknown ahead of time. The dogs had killed Kristin's last male a couple of years ago and she was hoping for Teddy's offspring now; it was hard to tell but she believed one of the females was pregnant.

She scraped the wood flooring, put back the removable board, and went to get bedding from the floor of the goat barn. The pigs were simple to care for. And Smoky, too. All he needed was some hamburger or milk-soaked bread or dog food for his breakfast meal. And she kept a newspaper in the bottom of his cage and tried to remember to tear a sheet off every day. It was the great nine-hundred-and-fifty pound one whom she loved best, that was a problem.

Kristin had a lot of problems; she put her mind off the chem test coming up on Monday. She had today and to-morrow to study for it; she felt that her dislike of math first of all, and chemistry next, was unequaled in the history of mankind.

She whistled, sounding almost as good as Mother. And she sang lusty-voiced when she knew Astrid was in the house and no one could hear:

> *He went from his palace grand*
> *And he came to my cottage door;*
> *His words were few but his looks*
> *They will linger forevermore!*

She was hitching the ungroomed mare to the Indian rig Danny had made. Her only solution to the horse's bedding had been leaves; a couple of times a week she went down into the woods for them, Bimbo and the setters sometimes following, to stuff burlap grain bags full.

About a month ago she'd stopped by to visit Mr. Was-ilewski, unhitching Blueberry and leaving her in the drive with the rein dropped. She'd knocked on the door. "I'm getting a supply against the time the snow falls," she told him.

"Come in and have tea." He didn't even have a dog or a cat.

He'd served the tea in glasses on his kitchen table cov-ered with brown butcher's paper in lieu of a cloth; with it he had a plate of soda crackers sprinkled with cinnamon and sugar. "Thanks."

Blueberry had followed Kristin up the porch steps, stumbling and clomping. And then she wanted to come inside out of the wind, to where the wood stove burned; she pawed at the door.

"Let her in," Mr. Wasilewski said. "Danny's mother used to bring a little horse she had into the house. That was before Danny ever came, and before things began getting hard for us."

The mare shuffled in and stood by Kristin's side while she sipped the scalding tea; Blueberry accepted a sugary soda cracker, spilling the crumb's on the floor and refusing another. She nudged the girl's shoulder. "Behave," Kristin said.

Mr. Wasilewski had a Bible on his lap. "This is Revelations."

"Go ahead. I like the Bible."

"And God shall wipe away all tears from their eyes and there shall be no more death, neither sorrow, nor crying, neither shall there be any more pain; for the former things are passed away."

"That's pretty."

"My wife stops overhead sometimes when she goes by."

Kristin nodded. "Danny told me."

Then Mr. Wasilewski had warned Kristin to watch out for fallen oak leaves which poison cattle. So after she'd turned the mare about in the small room, and they'd left, Blueberry skidding on the step, Kristin had looked for the shapes of leaves, for the mare often nibbled at her bedding.

That was weeks ago and Kristin hadn't had time to get back to see Danny's father again. As she headed for the woods now, the Farmer's Exchange truck drove up. Kristin had to rein in Blueberry and tie her to a post, the Indian rig still behind her, and go and dump up the grain.

Astrid sympathized, as she signed the bill for the men; she was in her school clothes and wasn't helping Kristin. "I'd loan you some straw, baby, but my bank account's just about nil." Astrid had got Margo's old assistant's job in the school principal's office. She was taking Daddy's Ford and going in to work overtime as she often did on Saturdays.

The sweat stood on Kristin's forehead. "Is the mail in yet?"

"I think so."

Kristin frowned; she'd got only one postcard from Danny and that was right after he left, addressed:

> *Michigan,*
> *United States of America,*
> *Western Hemisphere,*
> *The Earth,*
> *The Universe,*
> *The Mind of Man*

And next to it, in a scrawled pencil:

> *All they have are Holstein cows and hogs. Also two hired hands besides me. Uncle Jock is ONE BIG CRAB. Sincerely yours, Daniel W.*

She'd written back an involved three-page letter, telling about Blueberry, how for one thing she'd put the sidesaddle on and the mare hadn't minded at all, and then when they were cantering down the long dune slope that dipped sharply into the blow, the fragile leather girth snapped, and Kristin almost lost her balance. There was no use repairing it, but at least she knew the horse would take a saddle.

She hadn't heard from Danny since. That was two

months ago. Kristin wanted to write but felt it might be bad etiquette and daily looked for another card. She wanted to tell him about her days; Kristin had no other best friend. She was lifting the sacks and letting the grain pour into the big clean iron once-molasses barrels. The flour-like dust clung to her perspiring face and arms. When she'd finished she brushed it from her jeans and got her leather jacket. She ran to the house to see the mail.

There was an advertisement from a Chicago firm that sold swanky riding equipment; that was all. She leafed through it while she drank a cup of chocolate milk she made. Then she slapped together a peanut butter and strawberry jam sandwich and with it in her hand, returned to the mare. While she worked down in the woods she tried to recall the *Law of Mass Action*.

"Other conditions being the same, the speed of a chemical reaction is directly proportional to the concentrations of—something." She unfolded a grimy piece of notepaper on which the chief laws were scribbled. "To the concentrations of the substances reacting." She repeated the statement until she felt she had it memorized.

She preferred poems and, to rest her mind, declaimed one she and every person in school that was a horse lover knew all twelve verses of:

> *Fret not to roam the desert now*
> *With all thy winged speed,*
> *I may not mount on thee again;*
> *Thou'rt sold, my Arab steed!*

She trudged back to unload the leaves. In the weekend there was no time to ride.

Kristin had wanted to start Blueberry over some jumps, and she had been working on a trick where the mare went to a basket and brought it back, the handle in her mouth. Danny had outlined that one in her notebook; she mashed an apple in a cloth and when the mare learned to pick that up and bring it, Kristin tied the cloth around the basket handle. Blueberry was catching on. The basket was kept in the cave in the woods.

If she ever had a minute to spare for moping, she went and sat inside there, Smoky on a shoulder, Blueberry with nose dropped to the ground, gazing in at her. Sometimes Kristin wept, face down, in a long-drawn-out unforgiving unassuagable way. The tears were brought on by some minor incident or casual word, regarding something undefinable, unnamed, some loss that had not yet occurred, some desire not even known. And after a while she came out, her blue eyes softened. Blueberry nudged her, following as she scuffed back on the leaf-deep path in the darkening fall where there was no twilight, only day and then night.

At the barn she wasn't required to milk; that was Astrid's job. But she had the daily chores of hay to throw down, grain to distribute individually to the milkers, bucks and yearlings to feed. She was also to watch for does coming in season, to get them bred to the buck Astrid stipulated, keeping track on the calendar that hung in the small whitewashed dairy room. And she must gather eggs from the banties and scatter scratch, and give a wet mash and corn to the ducks and Astrid's young geese, change the water, bring warm water to the fowl when a film of ice formed as the air got nippy. She whispered the chemistry formulas to herself as she went about.

But when it came to the exam on Monday only one of the laws she'd learned by heart was asked for. Kristin considered it pretty unjust; all the kids were complaining on the bus home. They crowded together in the back. Astrid sat with the seniors behind the driver and glanced back annoyed when the littlest got too loud.

"I move we go on strike," Kristin shouted. The test questions had referred to the very newest material taken up in class, and Kristin never even heard of it. Fortunately Astrid wasn't like Margo whose favorite subject had been responsibility, and she kept still about the exam at home. Kristin was saved from having to go through a hazing at the supper table.

November ended and December started and the days went by. Then, shortly before Christmas, the week before vacation began, a guinea pig dropped a pair of babies, one white and the other red; their hair short like the mother. Lucky things always happen by sixes and sevens, and it never rains but what it pours, and so Kristin wasn't especially surprised to find a letter when she got home from school. She snatched it from the table and dashed out of the house to read it, still in her wool plaid skirt and knee socks and tweed car coat. She sat on the edge of the manger in Blueberry's stall.

"Wow," she told the mare, "he's coming."

Danny'd had his fill; his uncle beat him with his belt a few times when he stood up against him. And one night Uncle Jock made him stay outside as punishment, and Danny went to sleep with the cows. Uncle Jock could go soak his head in the hog trough. Danny was leaving, hitching rides south. He planned to see Kristin on the way. He ended:

Meet me in the cave where we used to play pirates when we were children. How is the buckskin nag? Did you ever think of breeding her? You could sell the colt easy; it's a good way to get some money. Go to the cave every evening this week. I'll hang a railroad engineer's bandana on the oak tree roots to signal I am some-where about. I remain your friend, Daniel W.

That evening Kristin began saving up food. In case he got there at once, she galloped down to the cave with a half-dozen apples. She hung them from the ceiling of the cave to save them from racoons and possums. She rushed through her work and after supper went out to Blueberry and groomed her well. There was an extension cord she'd run through a hole she bored in the barn wall, so she had a light in the stall.

The mare stood, quiet, even when Kristin worked with the curry comb on her tender parts, belly and loin and flanks. She finished with a brush and then an old turkish towel. She picked up the feet one at a time to clean the frog. Blueberry didn't look very flashy, she decided; her win-ter coat was such that she had a Teddy-bear look. Kristin groomed her head with the towel and said what she'd been thinking since the letter came.

"Would you like a foal, girl!"

All day in school she saw Danny in her mind, tramping down the path and knotting aloft the kerchief; in the eve-ning she pelted on the horse down the woods, scrambled over the creek bridge, the mare wading the icy water. But there was no sign. Astrid complained when she got back just before supper.

"I've had to do some of your chores over again lately, Kristin." Astrid's dark smock covered her school clothes. She was shelling ear corn for the three young gray and white geese who stood slender, inquiring, "Woo-woo-wooooooooo?" They picked up the orange grains.

"Darn, I'm sorry."

The gander hissed and wove his neck, snakelike; his cheeks puffed; delicately he accepted corn from Astrid's palm. "Just stop playing so much, Kristin."

"Say, I'm thinking of breeding Blueberry!"

"Good. Who're you going to use?" Astrid was stroking the goose's back feathers; he waited tamely on her, quiet.

"There's a stable advertises an Arabian stallion not far from Michigan City."

"Bet he costs a lot."

"I'm going to find out. I'm going to phone them up."

"Why don't you hurry and get the feeding done, baby? It's nearly dark."

"Okay."

Kristin planned her first words to say to Danny, "I'm going to use an Arabian stud!" She practiced the words as she pushed the hay down through the loft hole and then ran to the house to fill two pails of hot water for the poultry. Snow was coming in needling gusts as she carried the buckets, the liquid sloshing and chilling her pant legs as the wind rushed here and there. She was unable to do more than nibble at her supper, the feeling like a fever in her, wanting to see the boy.

Part of her excitement was that it was a secret. Astrid and Margo when they were about eleven and twelve, had devised a private language they spoke between themselves. They'd had code phrases that stood for certain things: *the cat is on the mat* meant Daddy's in a temper and watch out. *I'm crazy about five-four-time jazz* meant they were to meet behind the garage for consultation on some important matter. Kristin felt her aloofness now from her family; she lived in another land and spoke another tongue.

Mother patted her cheek as they left the table, "What's the matter, dreamer?"

"I know how she feels," Astrid said. "It's because vacation starts tomorrow and Margo's coming too!"

"Yeah," Kristin said. "And I've got an idea; I might breed my horse, too."

"Hush." Mother put her fingers to her mouth. Daddy hadn't heard and was already sinking in his chair with his book. "We'll talk about it tomorrow, dear. Don't bother Daddy. He's tired."

The next day the snow still came; the wind had fallen and the flakes were huge and soft. School let out right after the assembly program; drifts were already forming. Daddy went out in the early afternoon to sprinkle sand on the drive and to clear paths. Kristin waited until he was gone to phone the riding stable that kept the stallion. They were brusque with her, asking her age, and saying that the fee was $150, living foal guaranteed. That was without papers; with papers, $500. Kristin went to tell Mother who was serving the few customers as was her habit during the slack season. She was slicing a lamb roast with a skinny blade, the dry pale meat folding over, the pink juice flowing.

Kristin cried, "It's too high; it's not fair!"

Mother laid the thin slabs on her blue plates and spooned on each from the dish of thick lentils and onions. Mother loved the kitchen; she always basted her roasting lamb with a cup of coffee, with cream and sugar, that she poured in the bottom of the big roaster. "Daddy wouldn't let you anyway, dear. And I don't approve. Why don't you just enjoy your horse."

"Everybody squelches everything I want to do. Why!"

Mother took up the plates, preparing to carry them into the dining room. "None of us have the time to help if something went wrong. Suppose you lost your mare foaling? That could happen. Now run along, dear."

Kristin's eyes were a brilliant blue; she wanted to protest, but instead flung herself from the house taking with her the sack of sandwiches she'd hidden, Danny's favorites: strawberry jam and grape preserves. When she arrived at the cave she and the mare were dusted with the white flakes; Blueberry shook her name to clear it, shivered her skin. Kristin dismounted and gathered some dry leaves, pushing the snow aside to find them; she bedded the cave deep and hung a gunny sack she'd brought for a door. She slipped inside and it was cozy, almost warm. Field mice had been at the apples, nibbling, and Kristin didn't mind; she knew he wouldn't either. After a while she had to go; her work was being neglected.

For a week her impatience and fervor accumulated. Margo came home, a pretty stranger; it took a few days to feel familiar with her again. Margo spent hours talking with Astrid. The snow continued to fall, carpeting the pastures, woods and the paddock; frosting the barn and stable roofs, stacked tall over the cavy house and rabbit hutches. At night Kristin shut Blueberry up in the dark of the stall, and in the day, even if it snowed, she left the top of the Dutch door open. The mare hung her head out, stirred by the chill air; her coat was thick and her mane and tail were long.

Kristin rode the mare highstepping through the two-foot powdery snow that remained as the storm cleared. The sky was blue, the sun yellow, the temperature below freezing. The lake had frozen near the shore and icebergs built up in a series of steadily growing mounds as the waves charged over them. On the dunesides drifts were three-and-four-feet deep and Blueberry plunged at them, eager. She reared before she left the barnyard, standing tall, and then set out at a canter, snorting noisily in time to the rhythm of her gait. The wind circled, icy; Kristin wore mittens and a wool scarf up to her nose. The steam rose from the mare's breath and the girl's.

One evening at dark Kristin shut the mare in after brushing her up and covering her with a stable blanket she'd sewed from a red-and-black checked cast-off. She came into the entry and pulled off her boots and mittens, stood blowing on her hands and putting them over the hot radiator to warm them. She heard her sisters and Mother in the kitchen.

"Don't tell her, dears."

"I don't believe any experience should be kept from Kristin, Mother," Margo said. "That's what'll help her mature. Even unhappiness is good for people, I think."

"She doesn't run off to bawl anymore like she used to do," Astrid said. "Our Kristin's always happy; it's the horse."

"I know," Mother said. "But don't tell her. She's fond of Danny and I'm sure she thinks he's content up there on his uncle's farm."

"Mr. Wasilewski was upset when he told me," Margo said. "He didn't see Danny; they took him straight back to his uncle."

"The thing I don't like," Astrid said, "is the idea of the police picking him up hitch-hiking."

"As if he were a criminal," Margo said.

"Poor Danny," Astrid said.

"Now dears," Mother said, "I'm sure it wasn't that bad."

"Mr. Wasilewski doesn't look very well and he says he didn't have enough money for food and clothes for Danny. That's why he had to send him to his uncle's to work."

"The Community Circle brought him a Christmas basket last week," Mother said. "I made sure there was a ham in it, and sugar and coffee. Perhaps I ought to start dropping in on him now and then."

"Daddy can't stand those people," Astrid said. "Gypsies, you know!"

"That's only the boy," Mother was firm. "Mr. Wasilewski's not got a drop of gypsy blood. I'll tell Daddy so. I'm going to go calling next week. I'll just slip down there."

"Brave Mother," Astrid giggled.

"Dears, you make your nice jolly Daddy sound like some old ogre!"

"Our poor Daddy!" The girls joined in laughing.

Kristin was getting into her boots again, hurrying, awkward, her fingers and toes tingling, aching a little from being warmed. She opened the door as softly as possible and went out. Only near Blueberry, against the side of the dark stall, could she rid herself of tears so that she could face them at supper in the new role of one who was never a cry-baby.

"You're late," they said when she came in, stomping, rubbing her chapped hands, her cheeks scarlet, her eyes narrowed.

"So what?" She dared them.

One of Astrid's setters came to greet her, a large slice of home-baked yellowish bread in his mouth that he'd stolen from the kitchen table. He strode past, unguilty, and flopped down, a paw upon his food, looking around for his brother to follow, wanting to argue about it with someone.

"Kristin's thinner," Margo said. "Did you notice, Astrid?"

"I am not," Kristin blazed. "Let me alone."

"What're you getting mad at? What'd I say?" She

pointed at the Irish setter. "Look at your goofy dog, Astrid."

"I know," Astrid giggled. "He thinks no one saw him snitch it."

"I'm not mad," Kristin spoke, belligerent.

"Girls," Daddy said, "let us have peace."

"Okay," Margo said. "I can't wait till Astrid comes to State next year."

The second setter had trailed his fellow; they glared over the food that neither was hungry for; it was a token. Their lips twitched; their white teeth showed; their snarls quavered. "Sillies," their mistress said.

"We'll have a ball," Margo told Astrid.

"How many boy friends do you have?" Daddy asked.

"Four steadies," Margo boasted, and snapped her fingers softly at Bimbo who leaned against her chair on his haunches, his bushy tail thumping in response.

"Just stick to numbers," Daddy said, "and I'll feel safe."

"I'm not going to go to college at all." Kristin wanted to fight.

"You don't have to, dear." Mother patted her Mr. Shams who rolled his gold eyes up at her.

"For one thing," Kristin said, "I probably won't even pass this year!"

"Nonsense," Daddy said.

"I'm sure to fail chem. That's definite. I hate that teacher."

"Grades are given out in mid-January, aren't they?" Daddy asked, and Kristin felt the danger in his voice.

She bearded him, reckless. "All the kids hate that teacher. And I know I'll get *D* in math again."

Daddy looked at her. "Now Kristin, I don't know why

you're behaving in this childish fashion, but I'll try to stick to the subject. You recall what I told you: if you fail, you're going to have to sell your horse. First things first in this family. Understand?"

The littlest wouldn't reply but stared.

"I'm not going to look at the report card coming up, since you seem to know the grades beforehand. *Don't* study and *don't* take your tests if that's the way you want to look at it." Daddy got up, the head of the house. "I'm going to wait until June, when final grades are given out. C or better in every subject or Blueberry goes." Daddy walked out of the room.

Kristin felt like Chicken Little in the primer story, who was sure the sky would fall and gathered everyone to go to tell the king. Now the sky was plummeting about Kristin's ears.

VI

Dawn was firing

the east and all April flowers turned to face the arriving sun. Kristin, in barn jeans and an old loose sweater, a notebook under her arm and a paper sack in her hand, slipped out the back door and came to Blueberry's paddock. The mare went in and out of her stall at will now. The squeaking door swung open. The weather was fair. Blueberry was lying in the yard and lifted her head to watch the girl approach. Kristin knelt in front of her and the horse nosed the sack, tearing it open with her teeth, finding the bread crusts, apple peelings, the raw egg. She daintly cracked the egg first, lapping the contents as they spilled on the ground. Then she chewed on the rest while Kristin opened her notebook and began to study. The girl leaned back against the horse, sitting just behind the folded front legs in the soft-furred belly area.

It was only a little after five and she had nearly an hour and a half of undisturbed time before Astrid would come out to milk, and Kristin would go to her chores.

Sometimes Blueberry would stir and rise. The girl spoke to her, not lifting her head from her work. If the mare didn't return after a while she missed her and whistled and the mare came over slowly. She lay down of her own volition, or waited for Kristin to tap her front legs; then she sighed and buckled them under her, settling by the girl.

Sometimes if it rained, or the wind blew hard, Kristin sat reading, astride the horse in the stable; she pushed aside the spider webs that drooped from the crossbeams of the low ceiling. Smoky sat on her shoulder or on the side of the manger, unafraid.

Kristin had changed; in terror over losing the one she loved, she'd settled doggedly over the last four months to her books. In her new earnestness and sobriety, she made up rigid schedules so that she was also able to fit in time to school her mare, four hours every Saturday and the same on Sunday. And she stopped the lesson right on the dot. Blueberry had learned to walk sidewise without tangling her feet; graceful, she dipped her head and minced. Now she was practiced at rearing, and stood erect while Kristin was before here, the front hoofs gathered under, the legs glistening and dark, the mane and forelock waving, the almost-black tail streaming on the ground. Kristin had groomed out her winter hair, and kept the stable coat on her, and the buckskin coat was a golden silk.

Kristin had almost managed to put Danny out of her thoughts; the wrenching pain gradually eased as time smoothed it over. She looked sometimes for a letter, but felt his male rebellion. She knew Uncle Jock figured all boys were in need of subjugation, forgetting Danny'd had a taste of authority while he took over a man's role, caring for his father and the farm.

Kristin's fear of losing Blueberry and the resulting necessity for hard mental work as well as the steady turning wheel of chores about Margo and Astrid's little animals, helped her in getting used to pain. When she felt the wave that was loneliness for her friend Danny sweep toward her, she met it quietly, bearing the force of it, knowing that it would wash away in a day or so. She drove herself into her studies, leaning against the horse, her small hand feeling for the fur and it's comfort.

In the afternoon she rode briefly so the mare should not grow soft. Often she went down to the cave. It was a day in May and a springtime rain was falling, not a mist and not drops but something between. At first, everyone had thought there would be a rainbow. Mother had put out some flower seed after the noon customers were gone. She refused to come in when Daddy called. She knelt in a dream over the rows, her hair curling like a girl's in the moisture. The paper seed envelopes lay discarded and soggy, the dirt clung to Mother's hands and apron, on her cheek where she'd brushed her hand. Daddy shook his head and Astrid and Kristin knew he admired Mother.

"When she gets stubborn that way," Daddy declared, "no use to try to make her see any sense. She's like an animal that'll run straight back into a burning barn." He kept looking out the window in a soft, pleased way. He was repairing frames, and was kneading a ball of putty.

He tried to stop Kristin too. "You'll catch cold. Don't go out riding now!"

"I *have* to, Daddy. It's the only time I have." Kristin had changed from her school clothes into jeans.

"What do you mean?"

"I'm on a schedule."

"For what?"

"For my day."

"Let's see." He took the creased paper and unfolded it:

> 5:00 *Get up and wash face*
> 5:10 *Study*
> 6:45 *Start chores*

7:45 Breakfast
8:00 Dress, also wash more
8:15 Catch school bus
4:26 or 4:41 Return of bus. Ride till
5:00 Then do chores
6:00 Study till supper and after
9:30 Bed

"I've got another schedule, too," she said, "in my notebook which gives more details."

"So? Well." Helpless he watched her go off like Mother, dreamy, through the falling shower. Soon she was speeding on the wet mare bareback, toward the woods, her legs loose at the sides, her body adapted to the mare's movement.

A faded red railroad man's kerchief, draggling in the rain, was tied on high to the oak roots.

"Yeow!" she yelled, hurling herself from Blueberry.

Danny was asleep in the cave, the burlap door hooked out of the way. He opened his eyes and grinned. "Better late than never."

She was on her knees before him, the horse in the cave's entry, snuffling, a little alarmed. "Wow. Danny."

He scratched his head. "Nice and soft in here, Kristin. Did you get all these leaves just for me?"

"Yeah. And I got a blanket too, but I was afraid it'd get moldly and took it back. You going to stay a while?"

"Sure. I figure you can sneak me some food."

"I know!"

"The creek's nice and fresh."

"Yeah."

"And this weather suits me for loafing."

"Yeah."

"How've you been, Kristin?"

"Okay. You?"

"I'm okay. How's Blueberry?"

"She's okay too."

"Let's have a look." He went over the wet mare with his hand, thoughtful. He picked up her feet; docile, she shifted her weight as he examined them. "She's nice-mannered, Kristin."

"Thanks."

She saw how Danny was changed; he was older-appearing, taller, his clothes unfamiliar, the jeans tight-fitted and narrow-legged, his lumberjacket open at the neck. He was a stranger. He put his hand on the mare's flank and she switched her tail.

"Did you decide to breed her?"

"It's too expensive, Danny."

He turned to her, grinning again, his curls cropping out under the cap, his soft black eyes shining. "I wouldn't know you, Kristin. It's been less than a year but you're different. You're quiet, too. How come?"

She shrugged. "*You're* different too."

"Not like you." He reached out and pulled on her damp flaxen braid. "Maybe it's because you're fifteen now."

She flushed, drawing back. "So are you. Did they call you Daniel there?"

"Yeah. But why do you have to have an expensive stud for her?"

"I wanted an Arabian. Costs $150."

Danny got serious then. "A little quarter horse would nick nice with Blueberry. The colt would be worth something." He stroked the mare, like Kristin, hungry for the feel of the satin fur, the smooth flesh, warm. I'm thinking of a stallion the county agent stables somewhere near here.

It's his own horse and got nothing to do with the govern-ment. He'd bring him over and only charge you about ten or fifteen dollars."

"What's a quarter horse?" She was unwilling.

"And I've seen him. He's real nice, a chestnut sorrel."

"I never heard of a quarter horse."

"They're bred to race a quarter-mile. A long time ago they used to race them down village streets or wood paths. They don't look like a Thoroughbred that's supposed to run a long way on flat land. They're built low to the ground, a hand shorter than a racer, but weighing the same. They get away faster than any Thoroughbred and if the track's short, can beat him."

"I wanted a fancy horse, Danny."

"A quarter horse is fancy. They've got fast blood and still can get along on the feed that'd starve a Thorough-bred. And they're quiet-dispositioned too. They use them a lot out West; when a quarter horse stallion knows his business, you can let him handle cattle, just guiding him by the mane or some little halter. And you can lead one broken proper with a piece of binder twine. They like people and being ridden."

"Sounds just like Blueberry. She might have some of that breeding in her."

"She could. There's a lot of duns and buckskins in quarter horse pedigrees."

"What's his name?"

"And they have a disposition that's suited for trick horses, Kristin. Quiet and sensible."

"Has he got a name that you know?"

"Red Wolf. That's a family name. Yellow Wolf and Black Wolf were famous quarter horse racers."

"I'll bring it up at home again. I hope my grades are going to be all right; I have to get all C's."

"You having trouble in school?"

"Yeah. How'd you do up there, Danny?"

The young lines on his brow deepened. "That's one thing I hated: leaving school. I was doing all right. Now, Kristin, get busy and keep your grades up." He felt he towered over the girl, mature, bold, having struck out on his own.

About them the fog shrouded the woods, ghostly, changing its character, hiding what stood behind and making what stood before seem to come forward, larger, a little ominous. Boles of trees that had reared stark and black in the winter months when Kristin had run here for haven, now in the Eden of May covered their parts with young green; vague, they were wreathed in the mist.

The children stood in the woods with the mare, and the hands of time stopped for a while. It was the sort of moment that would come back in dreams the rest of their lives, as a comfort. The three were reunited and for the moment had no connection with the rest of the world. Tomorrow, Daddy, an outlander, might wield the power of an adult and take the mare away. And Men of Law might again lead Danny, the minor child, back to his foster home with Uncle Jock. Kristin might be lonely and hurt. But that was the future, another hour. Now she was patting Blueberry at the same moment that Danny was. Kristin recognized what was happening, and then she felt the handles creak and time again turned.

"It must be after five," she said. "I have to do chores."

"That's right. You better go. Some one might suspect!"

"Yeah!"

"I'll get some more shut-eye." He crawled into the cave.

"After supper I'll bring some stuff," she shouted.

And just before dark she came with the blanket scented with mildew, and Blueberry's red-and-black checked stable cover for an extra one. She brought bread and jam and cheese to make sandwiches, and a handful of sugar loaves from the dining room for desert, and milk in a battered carton. On her shoulder was Smoky. The mare came at her singlefoot while Kristin balanced the burden. She stopped before the cave and Danny took the stuff; he put the crow on a branch where it sat half-asleep, dull, its day over.

"He's for company," Kristin said, "and I got to get back to study."

"Go on." The supplies were heaped on the ground.

"Mornings I get up at five to study too," she explained. "I'm on a schedule and it's hard."

"Don't let me interfere," he said. "Bring me books to read if you can."

"Maybe you could coach me for exams a little?"

"Hey! Swell, Kristin."

She rode off, his shout following, "Thanks for the crazy bird!"

By the next afternoon he had taught Smoky to climb up and down a tiny ladder of twigs and vines, and to pick up a stick in his beak and bring it to Danny. As the days went by, Kristin spent her study time in the woods; she brought books and food, candles and matches, soap and a towel. On Saturday, in the four-hour period set aside to train Blueberry, she let Danny handle the mare. The small education Smoky had received had gone to his head, and he went about, his lace dragging behind, gathering twigs and delivering them to Kristin who lay on her stomach studying, one palm open to receive the bird's loot.

Danny had knotted the red bandana in the four corners and wore it for a cap. He was beginning Blueberry's training on a waltz, which was difficult; he reined her tightly, worked her in a choppy step in short circles to the left and then the right. After a while he quit and groomed her till she gleamed spun gold in the sun. He sang at the top of his voice:

> *A Spanish cavalier stood in his retreat*
> *And on his guitar played a tune, dear!*
> *The music so sweet, would oft times repeat*
> *The blessings of my country and you, dear!*

The horse stood in the sunrays that filtered between the trees; Danny'd made a crown of small leafed branches to hang about her ears to keep off wood gnats and flies. He went to the creek to wash, and splash the frigid water on himself. He flung the towel on a bush to dry, and straightened his hair with a broken piece of comb from his rear pocket. He made a fire to toast rolls to eat with soft butter and honey:

> *Oh, say, darling, say, when I'm far away*
> *Sometimes you may think of me, dear!*

He offered Kristin the first roll. "Remember when we went up on Bald Tom that time?"

"How many years ago was that!"

"Did you tell your family about wanting to breed her, Kristin?"

"Yeah, and Daddy says okay. At first he wouldn't talk, but then I told him if my grades are bad and he sells Blueberry, carrying a colt just increases her value. Astrid's loan-

ing me the money. Maybe I'll advertise and sell my guinea
pigs. I don't want to, but I hate to owe a debt."

"Don't decide right now," Danny advised.

"Okay."

They leaned back. Danny said, "That waltz trick takes
a long time to learn. Could take a year if she's slow to catch
on."

"Yeah. And better cut it out if she gets with foal too."

"That's right." Danny reached for another roll to toast;
his red kerchief cap perched sidewise on his curls.

She sighed, "You think I'll get all C's, Danny? Exams
are in ten days!"

"I don't know. Do you understand the stuff?"

"They never ask the things I'm sure of." She turned
back to her book.

That evening Astrid questioned Kristin, "Where are
you taking all the food?"

Kristin blushed, glancing up. "What food?"

They were sitting on the edge of the back porch. A
half-dozen of Astrid's Flemish Giant rabbits grazed in the
grass at their feet. Kristin gathered one up on her lap, black
and white spotted, the long ears flattened.

"I've been watching you, baby. Are you taking milk
and things over to Mr. Wasilewski?" Astrid took up a fawn-
colored rabbit; she stood maternal with her pet.

"So what if I am?" Kristin leaned and put the rabbit
down; it ambled away, and paused in the sun. She didn't
look at her sister. "So what."

Astrid sighed, "I have to butcher some of the rabbits
tomorrow. I don't care much for the job. A farm's all a
parade of birthing and dying. I'm always hurting baby kids;
burning off their horn buds or butchering them because we

can't raise them all." Astrid's round winter-white face was peaches-and-cream, and her soft arms were strong; her blond hair was mussed. "But still I want to be a farmer always, Kristin!"

"So what if I did?" Kristin challenged her.

"Well, I don't think you should is all. Mother visited Mr. Wasilewski a few times when it was cold, but she says now that garden is going in, it isn't a good idea; it's patronizing, too. Mother and I saw you going out this afternoon, baby. We shouted but you kept right on going."

Kristin's breath was short as she patted Mr. Shams who'd come to use her lap. "Okay, Astrid. I won't any more."

"It's like a balance," Astrid went on, stirred, "and there's nothing tidy about it. All the roses come at once so the house is full, every pan and jar and vase. And when the strawberries come, you set out bowls of them and eat nothing else!"

"I know." But Kristin hadn't listened at all; she rose and pushed the cat off her knees.

Astrid was consumed by her own dark thoughts, stubborn. "I'll always be a farmer though, Kristin."

Kristin walked away, leaving her sister to moon over the little flock of rabbits. She had been frightened and was more careful thereafter. She spoke to Danny of it. "What do you think?"

He told her, "I've got to be moving on anyway. I'd like to stay and see that stallion is all."

They were not so much at ease as the next week passed; Danny stayed close by the cave so if someone approached, he could slip inside. He kept his clothes out of sight and quit singing so loudly.

I'm off to the war, to the war I must go
To fight for my country and you, dear;
And if I be slain, you may seek me in vain!

From his lumberjacket pocket he brought out the pack of cards his mother had made. They played gin rummy and casino and Danny did card tricks and told fortunes. "You'll go on a long journey, Kristin. I see trees and water. Maybe you're going to cross the ocean."

"Can't you tell something that'll happen sooner than that!"

"You can't hurry cards."

"Did your mother tell fortunes?"

"She wasn't that kind of gypsy, Kristin. She was a niece of the king, the *crayi*, and she was proud. You remember that poster of her in the center of the ring and all those black stallions. Well, the *crayi* taught her that act."

"Wow."

"And she snapped her fingers and they knew to come to face her."

"Am I lucky to be your friend, Danny. Whatever would Blueberry and I've done!"

"Your turn to deal," he said, humming his tune.

"Tell me another story about your mother."

"How about the elephant Emir, and the big fire?"

"Okay."

"They thought they had fire-proof canvas, but a match or something started a bale of straw burning, and the whole stable-tent went up in flames. They got the horses out and the zebras and the camels and the mules. There were six elephants and five had been unchained and knew to run out when the fire began. But Emir was forgot and he stood in the middle of it all until the drivers missed him and went back to cover him up with wet blankets."

"Sounds crazy."

"And the ones that weren't hurt lined up in a row the way they were trained to do, trembling but not panicking. Emir cried like a baby. And they scraped off the burning skin while it was still on fire. He held still; nearly his whole right side was seared. But two weeks later he was back in the ring doing his act. My mother took turns with the other gypsies putting special salves on him."

"Wow."

"Next to horses, she liked elephants. And then bears."

"You make her sound alive, Danny!"

"Your turn to shuffle the cards," he said, humming his tune.

And then in the ending of May, about three weeks after Danny began hiding out in the cave, Kristin came running out one morning before dawn. There was a rosy cast to the still-dark air; the planet Venus, called the morning star, sat quietly dying in the same sky as the moon. As they went down the path, Blueberry threw her head, pulling on her lines, shaking her mane. Danny was still asleep and Kristin sat against a tree trunk with her geography until he emerged, stretching, yawning.

"Hi."

"The county agent's bringing Red Wolf over tomorrow."

"Yeah?" He went down to cup the creek water, drinking, spitting, flinging it over his face and neck. He returned, dripping, his black hair and shirt wet.

"Why don't you come down and get a look at him, Danny?"

"Say. I might. I'd like to see the shape he's in."

"What about using the tree house?"

They courted the danger. Danny grinned. "Suppose your Dad saw me!"

"Do it!"

They giggled, catching each other's eyes. "Officer, stop that man! Stop, sir. I say, stop, sir!"

"Come on, coach me on this dumb geography."

"Let's see. Now, Kristin, why does Uncle Sam wear red, white and blue suspenders?"

"Why?"

"To hold up his pants. What is the difference between the North and South Pole?"

"Who knows?"

"All the difference in the world. I'm afraid I'll have to give you an *F*."

"Then it's my turn. Why do ducks and geese fly north in spring?"

"Too far to walk."

"I wish I knew riddles easy like you, Danny. Sometimes I even tell them backwards."

"Like, what is the question for 'Because he's an ass'?"

"You're crazy. What is?"

"Why does a donkey like thistles better than oats?"

"Does he?"

"No, but it's a good riddle. Now let's get started."

The sun climbed slowly, hand over hand, into the day. As it neared a quarter-to-seven they put the book aside. Kristin had brought a chicken leg and Danny pulled it apart, chewing, giving Smoky the bone. Kristin lay on her back. Downstream a racoon was waddling to the water to wash a grasshopper he had caught, cracking the legs and pulling, with human-like hands, at the tissue wings; at the edge of the water he watched a fish for a while; with forepaw, he grasped at and missed one. In a bear-like shuffle, he went back into the woods to search for squirrel-homes to disrupt; for bird-nests to rob, sometimes catching a mother bird, a thrush or bobwhite who would not leave her clutch; and for bumblebee-nests to ferret from the turf for the honey and embryonic pupae.

On the banks of the ravine grew Solomon's-seal, the tall stems strung with tiny green bell-shaped blooms, and in damp sheltered spots, almost unseen, were yellow adders-tongue or trout-lily which lifted one pale flower within a pair of leaves that were mottled purple and white.

The quarter horse was due to arrive at ten the next morning. Danny was up in the tree house, concealed by the tattered canvas walls; he'd climbed there before the family woke, while it was still dark. Time went by; Kristin, hands in her jeans pockets, stood beside two white posts between which swung the *Blue Coffee Kettle* sign, watching down the highway. At a quarter-to-twelve she saw the little trailer, pulled by a black Olds. She waved to direct the county agent to the back of the restaurant to the barnyard.

The red-brown stallion stood sixteen hands, and had white stockings on his hind legs. He was a little fat, mild-appearing, his mane roached, his tail short, his coat satiny. He followed the agent down the tail-gate which was lowered for a ramp, slats nailed across it to give his hoofs purchase. Blueberry who was out of sight whinnied, and the stallion pricked his ears and curved his neck so the light reflected like water on it.

"Good morning, little lady?"

"Hi." Kristin led the way. "Come on."

The man was tall and angular, shrewd-eyed, sandy-haired, his dark pants soiled and loose-fitting, his white shirt sleeveless, cut off and hemmed at the shoulder. He whistled.

Every time I come to town,
The boys start kicking my dog around!

"That's her," Kristin said.

"Buckskin. That's the toughest color in horseflesh. Wolf's got plenty of buckskin in his pedigree."

"Hey!"

"I'd say your mare's going on four years, little lady?"

"She is." Kristin's heart thudded. "What's his pedigree name?"

"Fairview Red Wolf."

"Say. Can I pet him?"

"Sure. He's nice and fine-boned too. No bulldog like some. He's a race-type. Some fellow in Texas traded a hundred head of horses and mares for an ancestor of Wolf's. He might nick good with that mare."

"That's what a friend of mine thought!"

"That so? Now you hold his head for me, little lady. I want to move your mare out of the paddock."

"Okay."

Daddy came around the house to where she stood with Wolf. "Can I help?"

Kristin didn't want Daddy about; this was her moment; but she smiled, placatingly. "His name's Red Wolf."

"Want me to do something?"

"No thanks." The big horse pulled on the halter, obeyed her, "Ho."

"Why do you want a red color for the sire? Won't the foal be red? What do you want, Kristin?"

"I've got a friend says if it's a good horse it can't be the wrong color. And he says if you try to breed for a black filly and nothing else, you'll likely end up with a red horse." She was intense, facing him, rattling on, wanting to say her true thoughts: *Daddy, have you noticed I've been studying all the time!*

"I just heard about you going to the Pole's place

with food, Kristin. I was pleased to hear it. Mother's been there, and she told me about him. He's had a hard time. Mrs. Wasilewski was killed in a tragic way a few years ago."

"I know, Daddy." She was almost impatient. "She fell from a tree in their orchard; the branch was rotten. She used to work alongside Danny's father like a man; gypsy women do." Kristin spoke hastily. She wanted Daddy raking the stones in front of the restaurant, doing anything anywhere but here.

"I had no notion he was situated so badly, without food even. And he's a little off his head, imagines his wife comes to talk with him every day, too."

"At noon time," Kristin said savagely. "So what?"

"Well, I want to apologize for my attitude about those people. I hadn't thought out my prejudice."

Daddy glanced at the desperate littlest, his baby, holding the great bright beast with the curved clean-roached neck who leaned and gnawed at his lead and shook his head, the halter rings jingling. Daddy scratched his head, not tuned to his child, not hearing her unspoken words, *Daddy, what will I do if you take what's mine from me?* All he saw was the frowning child whom he supposed had done a womanly and generous deed.

The county agent was leading Blueberry down into the pasture and fastening her with a rope to a corner post. "You want to bring Wolf down here, little lady?" he shouted.

"Okay."

Daddy stayed in his tracks and watched Kristin going, composed and aware, leading the champing animal. She told the agent, "He's mannerly."

"Always been that way. He's got a grandfather was owned by a minister; he drove him to a buggy in the morning and preached, and then in the afternoon he ran him in the races."

Wolf pawed the ground and neighed, shrill, leaping the mare. His voice sounded far down into the woods where the tiny animals, possums or weasels or racoons, moved.

Blueberry pulled on her halter rope and Kristin untied it, frowning. "Do you guarantee a live colt?"

"Sure, little lady." The man took the stud's lead line. "And I've got to haul him clear up to Three Rivers this afternoon. I'm in a hurry all the time."

She reached in her pocket for the money Astrid loaned her. "Here's the ten."

"Righto."

She went to untie Blueberry. "Do I get a paper saying he's Fairview Red Wolf?"

"No, but I'll remember. I'm your county agent too, if you ever need your soil tested out in these fields and so forth." He shrugged. "Wolf had a nice mother, sorrel just like him, and worked without saddle, and even with a little colt by her, rounding the cows." He waved his hand, enthusiastic.

Kristin stopped him. "I sure would like to have something to tell that he's her colt's father." She gazed, Blueberry behind her, at the sleek well-fleshed mild red horse.

Daddy was approaching. "Haven't you been down here to test the soil once, for my older daughters?"

"Please," Kristin whispered, hurried. "I'd like it." She didn't know why it seemed a secret from Daddy. She wanted the moment to be her own, apart from the adult world.

"Well, write down your address." He fumbled in his shirt pocket and brought out a little worn notebook, *Red*

Circle Feed Almanac and Tables. "Inside the cover. It's not my rule, but I'll send you a paper to say."

She wrote the details, and then behind her Daddy was shouting, "Who's that!"

Turning, she saw Danny slipping down through the tall tulip tree and dropping light-footed to the ground. "I don't know," she stammered, as the boy lowered his head and ran, the pair of Irish setters spotting him and barking in pursuit; the boy raced for the fence, leaped it easily and disappeared into the woods.

Daddy was running and stopped at the fence, out of breath. He picked up the knotted bandana the dogs were sniffing. "Some tramp." Daddy turned to the girl who was following. "Got a notion to call the sheriff."

The county agent was fastening the tail-gate on the trailer and was gunning his car and rolling away. Kristin was wide-eyed. "I have to put Blueberry up, Daddy."

Daddy turned. "Did you recognize him? Is he someone from around here? How'd he know about that tree platform? I wonder if he's some friend of Astrid's? You girls wouldn't know anyone who'd wear a bum's cap like this! I don't like it a bit. I'm going to keep an eye open." Daddy marched up and down. "Dangerous!"

Mother came out on the back porch and called, "Are you busy, Daddy? Can you help us? We've broken the meat grinder!"

Daddy told Kristin, "Don't worry Mother about that fellow. I'll keep my eyes open. I'll take a walk down in the woods with the dogs. Maybe someone's escaped from somewhere. I'll listen to the radio. Don't you worry, Kristin."

"Okay."

She turned Blueberry into the lot and got a pitchfork to clean out the stall. All the time she worked her pulse thumped and she thought how he was gone now, and the world once more against him. Blueberry nuzzled her arm and she put the fork aside and began unknotting the tangles in the mare's mane. Sometimes the strands would rope and plait almost overnight; Danny said gypsies told that angels did it. And if horses were loose in pastures for a winter when it was time to comb them, one had to use a woman's heavy hatpin; it was the only thing to tease the knots free, starting at the ends and working up.

Kristin got on Blueberry, tapping her to make her kneel, mounting and riding at a slow walk. She had to go down to the cave for Smoky. She hated to go near there and blamed herself for cowardice, brooding.

The crow was not on its customary branch and Kristin went about the silent woods calling, "Smoky! Here boy." She clambered about the oak roots and up the ravine sides, here and there.

She felt the bird might have tried to follow the boy in the morning, getting free of the perch and thong. And then she came upon a scattering of black tail and wing feathers, telling where Smoky had been tricked by the racoon who'd come the day before to wash his insect in the creek. She saw in her mind some prowler who circled round and round under Smoky's perch, the crow following the movement, until dizzy, he tumbled, fought, and was carried away on the shoulder of the yellow-eyed thick-furred beast. Kristin hunted about the woods for a long time searching for more evidence, and then went homeward.

In the green-lit pathway she vowed, "I'll get another crow first chance I get. I'll call him Smoky and teach him everything Smoky knew."

She wanted to bend fate her way. She tried to make what had happened not have happened. She set her mind, stubborn, refusing even the tears that fell. Her legs were tight about her mare, her blue eyes bluer.

the porch, watched customers' cars pull off and go down

❧ ❧ ❧ **VII** ❧ ❧ ❧

Kristin, standing on

the porch, watched customers' cars pull off and go down
Highway 12. She could hear their voices going on and on
in the kitchen. "And in fall she ought to be able to raise
this C to a B," Daddy was saying. "After all, Margo's her
sister and getting A's first year in college."

"Yes, dear," Mother said.

But Margo wanted to argue. "I don't think our Kristin
can *do* any better than C, Daddy."

One thing, Kristin thought in quiet joy, Blueberry's
safe. She'd worn her sweater backwards for safety's sake,
and crossed her legs, and everything was C, but her usual
B in English. She went down the steps, heading for the
patches of vetch growing in the ditches along the roadside.
She pulled handfuls of the legume, purple flowered, and
when she had a stack, carried it to the rabbit hutches, stuff-
ing the center feed racks; she gave Blueberry a handful and
the rest she put in with the cavies who squeaked as she approached. It was fragrant and the little pigs burrowed into
it.

She caught the white long-haired Teddy and while he
nibbled on the green, sat him in her lap and began to comb
him out. She was entering him in the little county fair
again this year, just for fun. It started tomorrow and her

sisters were about ready; the goats were sheared, their hoofs trimmed, the trailer readied. Astrid had made show blankets and the little animals would wear them, white with green trim, and *Margastrid Herd* scrolled across both sides.

"Hold still, boy," she told Teddy, the excitement turning about in her. Kristin was convinced she'd find Danny at the fair; she felt he'd be working for the derby-hatted ringmaster who'd sold her Blueberry. She looked forward to seeing the string of horses, Ginger who was Blueberry's mother, and Hurricane and his act. She had no desire any more to ride the broncos or the bucking ponies. That was for children. She wanted to swagger in back of the tent and greet the man and ask if her gypsy friend was working there. The thing, like a bird, fluttered in her and she sighed with impatience.

The guinea pig's silk hair glistened in the June sun; she put him back hoping he would stay clean and not tangle too much before the next morning. He ran into the vetch and it clung to him. "Ugh, Teddy."

Her sisters, jean-clad, were hurrying into the goat barn. Kristin wandered over to Blueberry's paddock to groom her and to listen to her sisters' talk through the barn window where they brushed their goats and tended last minute chores. "Some of the boys are coming through this summer," Margo said, "and they're dying to meet you."

"You know how I am about blind dates," Astrid said.

"Everyone will be cute," Margo promised. "You can have the cutest if there's a difference."

"Don't forget," Astrid giggled.

"I wish you were coming to State this fall," Margo said.

"For the sake of fun, me too," Astrid said. "But it makes more sense to go to a secretarial school close by.

You know, when it came to enrolling in State and facing leaving the Nubians and even my geese, I couldn't do it. I want to stay on a farm always; I think I can make a living at it, along with some office job. The school principal says I can work for him as long as I want."

"How did our Kristin do in the winter, Astrid?"

"No complaints. Baby's in love with her horse."

"That's the way they all are at her age. Till they trade them in for a man."

"I don't think Kristin ever will," Astrid said. "She's like me; the only man I marry's got to be as crazy about goats and geese as I am!"

"I'm going to write that down and make you sign it," Margo said.

"I want to buy about ten acres of that land bordering us in back, Margo. This place is too small for the kind of purebred herd I'd like to keep; I want to make a few top milk records for the country and get a name in the industry. I might even import from England; I've written to a herd there. I want a buck kid out of a champion they've got. His mother's a champion and he's got three champion daughters."

"Let's go halves, Astrid."

"That's what I was hoping you'd say. Do you think you'll stay in the business with me?"

"Sure. We're the Margastrid Herd."

"Sometimes I think you'll meet someone at State and never come home," Astrid giggled. "You know I've registered the prefix Margastrid with the American Milk Goat Record Association. I hope your boy friends will understand why you can't go off and marry them."

"I'm crazy about men," Margo sighed. "I like to be babied."

"You're lost," Astrid said. "Not me."

"I like to be spoiled; I like to boss boys around."

"I just want to buy land. And that's what I want to talk to you about next, Margo: land."

"I never thought about it."

"Remember Danny Wasilewski?"

"Sure, is he still working up north for his uncle?"

"No, he ran away again a month ago, around the middle of May, and the police have had a lookout ever since. This time they want to return him to his father."

"How come?"

"Guess."

"Mr. Wasilewski got some money from somewhere? Did he marry again? Or did the gypsies leave Danny a fortune?"

"Neither, but it's just as good, Margo. Now listen. You and I are going to have to get some money."

"How?"

Kristin, taking the vines of vetch, was plaiting the purple flowers in Blueberry's mane. The mare nibbled on the ribbons at the girl's braid ends; the two stood as if sleepy in the sun, but Kristin was attending. "Ho, girl," she whispered.

"I don't want Daddy especially to hear," Astrid said, "because he thinks we're about nine and a half years old and always will be. I'm tired of being a minor. I can't wait till I'm twenty-one."

"What's the plan?"

"We've got to get a loan quick to buy that land behind us. A real estate company's snooping around here and buying up property, for one, the Wasilewski's."

"No kidding."

"He kept the house for himself and fifteen acres of

orchard and garden. They only wanted his duneland; they're
going to put up summer cottages."

Margo asked, "How much do we need?"

"A thousand right now, because it's not bordering the
lake. It's bound to get picked up pretty soon. There'll be
another real estate company here before long, I know."

"How are we going to get a loan, Astrid?"

"Why don't you work on Mother, Margo?"

"I'm pretty good at handling her."

"She'll side with Daddy; she always does."

"We're off to the war," Margo sang, "to the war we
must go."

"My pal," Astrid giggled. "Poor little Daddy hasn't
a chance. Let's make the frontal attack after lunch."

"Right," Margo said. "Say you remember that tramp
Daddy almost caught a couple of weeks ago, up in our tree
house? You think that could have been Danny?"

Astrid said, "Mother and I thought it might be him
trying to see Kristin. But Daddy says no; this fellow was
tall and skinny and went over the fence like a rabbit. Daddy
scouted in the woods for him with the setters and Bimbo."

"No! I'd love to see Bimbo protecting Daddy."

"Dumb old Bimbo. He's missed you, Margo."

Restless, waiting for morning when she would go
along to the fair with her sisters, Kristin got her swim suit
and went to the water. Since Margo was home she wasn't
required to help with the regular barn work and had time to
work on her mare. She still held to the pattern of her
schedule, schooling the mare where before she had put
time on studies. And she was reading poetry now, sometimes taking a paperback *Leaves of Grass* or an anthology
in her pocket as she went out on the horse. Now and then
she sat by the cave where she had spent the space of time

with her best friend, which seemed now to encompass years.

As they waded into the water, Blueberry paused to drink. Kristin paddled her feet and waited. Then she urged, "Up, girl." The mare reared like a little fabled animal, standing a moment, hoofs outstretched, before plunging down. She, on command again, reared, the water dripping foaming from her hoofs. They went out further and while the mare waited in the cool, Kristin dived from her, swimming far, open-eyed under water. She found a stone and, standing on the horse, hurled it, plunged after, trying to exhaust herself, swimming at full strength and speed, always. Before they went home, they swam far out, past their depth, Kristin almost deliberate in her desire to feel danger.

The mare could easily be unbalanced when out deep, unable to get purchase with her feet on the sand floor. Her head and her neck's crest, like a mythical beast, was visible, the dark mane floating out. And behind, like its mate, the head and shoulders of the girl, sometimes astride, holding to the ribs with her legs to keep from floating up; and sometimes trailing beside, a hand on the mane so she was dragged along, the wake swirling. Only the pressure on the rein kept her paddling outward because Blueberry turned instinctively to the land. Finally they came to where the mare touched bottom. Kristin urged her to a trot; the foam splashed about the powerful beast, cascaded up on Kristin. Galloping, they returned up the sand hills.

At the barn, Margo and Astrid had a new emergency; there was another doe in trouble; this one had had her twins last week. She was Cleo, pitch-black, had won two Reserve Champions and one Best Nubian Udder at the shows. The twin kids were well, but the doe, for some reason, had not recovered. She was isolated and for draft protection wore a bathing suit, red, white and blue striped, fastened with safety pins on her belly.

The girls were feeding Cleo a pan of white warm milk just stripped from another doe. She dipped her head in and sucked, her eyes a little sunken, gazing on her mistresses. Kristin came to watch.

"We want you to take care of Cleo while we're busy at the fair."

"I'm going with you." They felt the aggression in her voice.

"Sure, baby," Astrid said. "In the aft I'll come back for you like last year. Okay? About two o'clock?"

"I want to go in the morning."

"Please," Astrid said.

Margo, practical, offered, "We'll give you two bales of straw and a bucket of ear corn."

"Okay." Kristin sighed.

In the morning, they drove off. Kristin, in the barn, leafed through her anthology in the black doe's pen, the doe's head in her lap. Cleo dozed, not willing to rise to her feet anymore. Kristin knew she would die and the girls did too; but Kristin didn't say it and they were unwilling yet to face it. She read about death, whispering:

> There is a beast that waits outside the door,
> Coughs occasionally, nothing more,
> Makes no bark no threaten no roar,
> I fear him so I weep at night.

Kristin rose carefully, adjusting the animal's head, placing it on the straw pillow; she went to get a kid feeding pan and walked out into the pasture. Kneeling by Sophie, she half-filled the container, white-foam topped. She brought it back to Cleo; the animal put her head in, oblig-

ing, but was unable to drink. Kristin took the pan out to
Blueberry who sucked eagerly, her first milk since baby-
hood; she didn't hesitate. Then Kristin pulled carrots from
a row, washed them at the water trough, threw them into
the paddock feed box. The mare dug at them, cracking off
pieces, crunching noisily.

Kristin told her more of the poem before going back
to the sick one:

> *This menace hidden from all sight,*
> *This mythological parasite,*
> *Has my undoing for his delight;*
> *I stir the fire to make it bound and glow.*

Poetry was almost a necessity to Kristin nowadays; she
fed on it, avid, needing expression and wanting her tongue
to feel out the syllables of her mother language. Kristin
was almost secret about her reading, kept the anthology,
with the bandana folded about it, hid.

She stroked Cleo's long black ears, silken, and thought
about her friend whose red kerchief was about the book:

> *I need a blaze to kill all shadow;*
> *Whatever burns on the flames I throw,*
> *And when the fuel is gone into the dark I'll go*
> *To the beast that softly coughs outside the door!*

Kristin was waiting in the restaurant's front drive for
Astrid. "Let's go! Mother's watching Cleo; she'll look in
every now and then. But it's no use."

"I know," Astrid said. "Why do I always hope against
hope?"

"She could pull out of it."

"No."

"I know. Did you win anything?"

"Margo's asters got a blue. We didn't expect it. They haven't even been hoed this spring! They came up from last year's seed."

She dropped Kristin off at the gate and the girl went running down past the sideshows, looking for the canvas tent. There was a ferris wheel and a carnival children's concession where it had been. She inquired of a barker, "You know where the horse acts are? Is there a rodeo this year?"

"Yes, ma'am. Come on in and take a look at my snakes first. I got everything from a boa constrictor to an imported poison asp!"

But she had gone. She discovered that the rodeo was only a minor affair, ten horses, scrubby ones; they didn't have a tent but performed behind a circular tarpaulin wall. "What's that name again, honey?" the dark wiry roughneck asked.

"Daniel Wasilewski."

"We had a Danny with us in April or May when we were working but he was near fifty, I'd estimate."

"This one's fifteen going on sixteen," she said. "Try and think if you've seen him."

"He your brother?"

"Yes," she said wildly, feeling he was; Danny was her twin.

"What kind of name is Wasy-loo-wiz? Sounds Russian to me."

"It's Polish."

"What's the difference, honey. All those names sound Red; *wiz* and *ski*."

"It means the same as *son*. If Thomas Jefferson was born somewhere else he'd have been Thomas Jefferski!"

"Hold on, honey, don't get so mad."

She looked at the various horses, each tied to a stake in the weedy field. "That's a scroungy bunch of nags."

The man shrugged. "They look pretty good in action."

But she wanted to fight. "I wouldn't own one of them. Not if you gave it to me."

"Nobody's going to, honey. Now you run along and play with your dollies. I've got work to do."

"I wouldn't take one if you paid me!"

He shoved her arm, "Move, honey."

"Let me alone." She hit his hand from her, hating his touch.

"Crazy brat," the man muttered and walked off.

Kristin didn't even see him go; she blamed herself for building a dream. Desultory, she went to hang around the goat pens, watching the Nubians while her sisters set out to see the sights. "I'm ready to go whenever you are," she told them. "I've seen all I care to see. It's a dumb fair this year, if you ask me. I'd as soon go home and take care of Cleo."

The summer dropped its days off in its honeyed way; Cleo died and was buried near the woods, a marker set up by the elder sisters. "I can't figure out what was wrong," Astrid said at the supper table.

"I'm glad we got those kids out of her," Margo said.

"I'm going to be a vet," Kristin said firmly. "That's what I'm going to study for."

The family turned, startled at the declaration from the littlest. Daddy raised his eyebrows, "Well, well."

"You do what you please, dear," Mother said, "but it's nice to know what you want early enough. Then you can slant your studies in the right direction."

"Where you going to school?" Margo asked.

"State has one of the best veterinary departments in this country," Kristin told her.

"That's so," Margo said. "I go with a vet student."

"Is he cute?" Astrid said.

"Yes. His name's Doc, and he'll be here in August when the Tri-County Fair's on. He's showing Southdown sheep and he knows everybody in the sheep barns."

"So little Kristin's growing up," Daddy said.

"Don't say it that way, Daddy," Margo objected. "Did you think she'd be a baby forever? You sound patronizing."

"Daddy's right," Mother said. "Our Kristin isn't a child any more."

"Old Doc Kristin." Astrid winked and kicked her under the table.

But Kristin shrugged. Not one of them had any idea of her determination; she felt that nun-like, she was dedicated. She'd go around curing animals. She wanted to handle big and small, every kind of beast she had time for. And she'd build up a string of trick horses too, and maybe raise some colts if she felt like it. The possibilities were endless. She wondered where Danny would be by the time she'd done all those things, when they both were old.

"Can I borrow Blueberry?" Margo was asking her.

"What for?" Kristin was shaking her head. "No."

"I don't mean now," Margo said, "but when this Doc comes by in a couple of months. I told him you had a horse and he knows a farmer near here with a big gelding he'll rent, and we want to take a picnic up on Bald Tom one day."

"Blueberry's carrying a foal."

"My gosh, she's just started. And Doc knows all about that, too. He's going to be a vet."

"Well, let's wait and see."

And then in August she liked Doc pretty well; he was short and squinty with kind hands and nothing but praise for the buckskin mare. And so when he swore perfect behavior Kristin said maybe, and when he asked if he could send her the old first year vet books that he had no use for any more, she just about had to say yes. She watched them leaving, the lunch in a rope sack hung from the pommel of Doc's old army saddle. He wore khaki and was mounted on a huge brown gelding; Margo in faded jeans and a silk orange shirt appeared tiny on Blueberry's bare back.

All morning Kristin brooded, wishing she'd stuck to no. She went to the kitchen and took Mr. Shams on her lap. Thunder was rattling in the west where storms came from. "Mother, you think they'll come back if it rains?"

"I doubt it, dear."

"I'd get in a cave or under a tree."

"A picnic's fun when there's a storm. I remember Daddy and I used to go."

Kristin couldn't believe it. "No!"

"You think Daddy wasn't just as entertaining as Doc and twice as handsome?"

"I can't think of Daddy as ever young."

"We don't exactly think of ourselves as old nowadays, dear." Mother rubbed her nose against Kristin's, pulling her ears.

"Mother, I love you." The littlest felt like telling her about Danny and the cave and how she hadn't given the supplies to Mr. Wasilewski in the spring. And how every now and then she let grownups accept a lie for truth and truth for a lie. And how she felt allied, the children against the elders, and often when the young increased their ranks with their pets, it became the children and the animals united against the adults; it was war; world against world.

She knew she was approaching adulthood, in just a few years would leave the land of children. She wondered when she'd forget the difference between the worlds. She said nothing to Mother now, patriotic to her kind.

The rain bumped on the window glass in slow thick drops; the storm would build its humor for an hour before it would really rage, upsetting the inland sea a mile away, dashing the sand about, tearing tree branches and leaves from their parents and filling the creeks to overflow so they'd wash up on the banks and all dry living things would have their thirst satisfied. Kristin stood up and put Mr. Shams in the warm place on the stool. He curled up at once and settled; Mother watched him, fond, and Kristin left, striding through the sultry uneven air under the blackening clouds that shifted and swirled in the wind tides.

She helped Astrid gather in the goats and close the barn doors on them; she let down the canvas shades on three sides of the tiered rabbit hutches; she shooed the skittery bucks, made playful by the cool wind, into their quarters. Then she went to help Astrid at brushing the Nubians that were selected for the show, oiling their collars, readying for the Tri-County Fair in two days.

She heard the storm lull for a moment, and then a streak of lightning cracked and in a moment a blast of thunder shook the barn. Astrid said, "Bet that got a tree."

"Wow." Kristin went to the door to let in the dogs, cowering at the entrance, shielded by the little roof, but seeking comfort from the gun-like sounds echoing everywhere. The two red setters and the old collie slunk in the corner, respectful of the goats who sometimes drove them about the yard, heads down as if they wore horns. The dogs knew their duty and merely avoided the animals, wagging their tails, eyes hopeful.

Then Bimbo, who was almost deaf, barked sharply and left the other two, his shaggy white head lowered, ambling to the door. He snuffed under it. "You suppose that's Margo?" Astrid said.

"I hope they took Blueberry easy." Kristin opened the door.

Thunder roared again and sheet lightning flashed everywhere making corners clear; the shapes of black-lined clouds stood out brilliant. There were odd colors in the storm-waged sky: green-yellows and purples, no color seen on a quiet day. The lightning sent a photo-like image to Kristin's brain and she peered into the rain that fell gray, to see if it were true.

At the gate she had seen one horse only, Blueberry, led by a boy in a drenched black jersey and ragged blue jeans, cut off below the knees; he looked like Danny Wasilewski. Following the horse was Doc, naked from the waist up. And on the mare's back, the figure of Margo, strangely stiff and prone. Bimbo had rushed by Kristin out into the yard in his limping hustling fashion, going to meet them.

"What's the matter?" Astrid looked up from the doe she straddled, a jack-knife in one hand paring a hoof.

"Hey, Margo's hurt!" Kristin passed the dog, running. "Danny?"

The boy seemed exhausted, face white, a cheek scratched with red lines. "Call a doctor, Kristin. Quick."

Kristin was leaping up the back porch and into the kitchen. "Mother, a doctor!"

And Mother was on the phone, and Kristin was outside again. Astrid was at the mare's head by the porch steps, and Doc and Danny were unstrapping the girl bound to the mare with wood vines, her left leg fastened to a stake splint with more vines and Doc's stripped knotted khaki shirt.

Margo's orange silk blouse was drenched and clung to her, and her hair fell wet out of the bun shape, the pins lost; her eyes were shut and her mouth was loose.

Nobody was crying; everyone was calm; Daddy came. He and Doc carried Margo who was recovering consciousness and beginning to moan, "Mama. I can't stand it. Mama," as they went up the stairs.

"Put her here, dears." Mother had laid the flowered pink sheets back.

They left the splint on because Doc insisted, although Margo protested that it was what hurt too much and must be eased. Daddy leaned over his lovely eldest and held her hand. "Darling."

"Don't leave me, Daddy."

"Darling!"

And the doctor was shouting down below, "Hey up there!"

"Kristin," Daddy stuttered.

And she ran to let the doctor in and lead him up. Danny stayed in the hall outside the room. Kristin joined him, leaning against the wall, unspeaking, eyes down. The doctor was talking to Margo and soon everything in the room, but for his voice and movements, was still. Kristin prayed for the eldest; she could feel how her mare was standing below in the downpour, unloved and wondering; Kristin was helpless to move to go to her. She had betrayed her horse, allowing strangers' hands to touch her, to sit upon her, and to be with her in a crisis. She felt gratitude to Danny who had filled Blueberry's need where Kristin had failed. Jealousy touched her in a kind of sickness. The lump remained in her throat. All she could do was wait.

Doc came out, hugging his bare chest, squinting at Danny, "Hi, hero. She's had a shock, but it's not a complex break, and he did a nice job of setting the leg. Any coffee around this restaurant, Kristin?"

"This way."

Danny followed. "*Caramba.*" He ran his hand through his wet black curls.

Kristin looked back as she went down the stairs. "What happened!"

"I was heading for the cave, Kristin!" Danny cried. "Why?"

"First things first," said Doc.

Kristin led them to the old-fashioned kitchen where Mr. Shams sprawled across one counter top and a tall blue-enameled pot of coffee stayed hot on the back of the great white stove. Doc got a blue and white cup from the shelf and poured coffee in it. He filled another for Danny, and glanced at Kristin who pulled on her wet long braid. "I hate coffee," she sighed, "but I'll take a little."

Doc gave her a cup. The cat rolled on his back on the counter as Danny rubbed his stomach. Kristin stirred lumps of sugar into the steaming fragrant fluid. Doc chinked his cup rim against theirs, nodding. "Cheers. Toast to Blueberry."

Kristin swallowed and set the cup down. "How come?"

"The heroine of the hour. Your friend here's the hero. I never saw anything like it."

"Tell."

"When the storm began we thought we'd take shelter under a cliff Margo knew. We had to climb to get up to it and lead the horses. Then Margo slipped off on the creek side, and I went tearing after, and the silly plowhorse ran away with your mare on his heels."

"That's when I came along," Danny said, as Mr.

Shams got to his feet, yawned, stretched, and leaped to the floor with a thump. "I heard Doc bellowing at them."

"I thought we were goners," Doc said. "Your sister was yelling like fury so I knew she wasn't dead, but I nearly panicked."

"I'd been having a nice day," Danny said. "I was cutting cross-country, going to look at the cave, and then slip over here and let you know I was working at the Tri-County Fair this year. My bunch already has their tent up."

"Call this a nice day?" Doc sipped the coffee. "Let's get a hot bath, hero."

"I'm nuts about storms," Danny said. "I heard him yelping, Kristin, and a great brown nag came bolting past and then Blueberry. I called out and she stopped dead in her tracks. I didn't recognize her till she put on her brakes. Then I whistled her over."

"I saw him coming over the head of the bank, sliding down, the horse alongside. Like a pair of angels."

Danny grinned. "I ripped his shirt up and tore off branches like he told me to for the splint, and pulled vines."

"And then he told your mare to lie down," Doc said, "and she knelt and settled right there in the swamp and leaves. She got up nice and easy with Margo and we fastened your sister on her. I never saw a mare the like of that one. Where'd she learn all that?"

"I showed her; she's smart."

"You did?"

"I know how; I learned from Danny."

"I'll never get over it!"

Kristin was restless. "I've got to go. She's out in the rain."

"Come on," Danny said.

"Can you feature where I'd be without that horse

today?" Doc asked as they turned to go. "Thunderation!"

Mr. Shams came skittering back into the kitchen to announce Daddy's arrival. Danny nearly bumped into him; in confusion he backed away, stepping on Kristin's sneakers.

"Hey. Look out."

Daddy stood tall, frowning. "You're Danny Wasilewski?"

"Yes sir." Danny had crimsoned, but held his ground.

"Well." Daddy's eyes were wounded, and they wandered over the room, to rest on Doc. "How about a cup of coffee, Danny, like Margo's friend?"

"Yes sir." Danny stood in front of Kristin. Both were poised as if for flight, as if each held his breath.

"He had some, Daddy," Kristin said. "And so did I."

"Well." Daddy's face was tense and anxious. "He ought to have a hot bath then."

Doc set his cup down with a little clatter. "That's what I was telling the hero. Here I go." Doc went by them and down the hall, whistling low.

The clock ticked loudly in the silence. The huge cat jumped on a stool and settled, kneading his tufted thick-furred paws, blinking his gold-flecked eyes, purring as noisily as the clock tick.

Danny said suddenly, overloud. "Thanks. But I ought to go. I've got a friend picking me up about five o'clock. I said I'd be out somewhere along Highway 12."

"He's liable to catch a cold, Kristin," Daddy said. "Let me put something on that scratch on your cheek anyway."

"Danny never gets a cold." Kristin spoke lovingly to Daddy.

"No." Danny shuffled his feet, shrugged. "It's okay, sir."

Daddy ran his hand over his face in a tired way. "I

don't care if you ever want to come around here, Danny."
He put his hand on the boy's shoulder, on the damp black
jersey. "Any time. I'm proud to know you."

"*Caramba.*" Danny grinned up at the man.

"Wow, Daddy," said Kristin. "Come on, Danny.
Blueberry's out there waiting!"

They dashed down the hall and out the door.

The mare was standing where the reins had dropped,
head low in the water that descended as if poured from a
tub. The noise and lights had stopped and there was only
the gray curtain of rain. As the pair came out, she moved
forward with a low nicker, ears pricked, head out. She followed them to her stall. Kristin made a hot mash and while
Blueberry ate with heavy chomping noises, the two rubbed
her down with sacks, drying her dun coat.

Kristin began combing out the long mane and tail,
unsnarling it with her fingers, and Danny went to the house,
bringing back a pail of warm molasses water. Kristin held it
up. The mare sipped, slobbered and gazed, her brown eyes
looking into Kristin's blue ones.

"Toast to you," Kristin said. "Cheers."

"Yeah," Danny said. "And I think your old man's not
so bad after all."

She blushed. "Mother's been talking to him. She visited your place this winter."

"Yeah? Well, I like him, Kristin."

"Say, when are you going home, Danny?"

"I haven't told you yet, but I'm not staying here any
more. I'm not going home at all."

"But now you can, Danny. I wanted you to know. I
didn't have your address and couldn't write about it."

"I'm working with horses the way I want to. With the
gypsy tribe. I'm staying at this job always; it suits me."

"But your dad has money now, plenty. And he wouldn't send you back to Uncle Jock's."

"I heard about him selling that land. And that's why I don't have to go to him, Kristin. I don't even want him to know I'm around."

"What about school, Danny?"

"See, he can get along without me fine now. He was my only real worry."

"He needs you to help, Danny."

"No. He likes truck-farming; it's not for me."

"You *have* to go to school, Danny."

"You want to meet the *crayí*, Kristin? He's my granduncle."

"Where have you been, Danny? Where did you go when Daddy saw you getting down from the tree house? Were you scared?" She wanted every detail.

"I've been all up and down the country, Kristin, till I ran into these *gitanos* and they took me in! The fair begins day after tomorrow. You come to the gypsy camp behind the carnival tent and ask for me."

But she knit her brows as he dashed away and disappeared. She told Blueberry, fierce, "He *ought* to go to school."

❦ ❦ ❦ VIII ❦ ❦ ❦

The next day

Mother was in the kitchen clearing the coffee her way with egg whites; her voice came up the stairs.

A-swinging in the lane, a-swinging in the lane
I'd rather be with Rosie Nell
A-swinging in the lane!

Kristin was to go to the Tri-County Fair in Margo's place to show the Nubians in the ring, to care for the banty entries and the Muscovy drake and trio of ducks; they decided to let flower arrangements go altogether, this year. Bimbo was permitted on Margo's bed; Mother had put a bathroom rug at the foot and he was told to stay on it. His tail beat upon the coverlet as Kristin entered the room followed by Doc, bearing his guitar and a box of bonbons tied with a wide yellow ribbon.

Margo accepted the candy and offered some to Kristin. "They sure never would take you for my sister, Kristin. Can't you scrub up a little for tomorrow? Why don't you file your nails and put on some polish for a change? And don't braid your hair for the rest of your life. You're fifteen. Comb it back and tie it with this ribbon like those ballad singers do."

"And use my guitar," Doc said, "for effect."

"I'm me," Kristin chewed on a raspberry cream. "But I'll go wash my hands."

Doc hit his guitar, beating out a syncopated rhythm and then running over the strings. Margo and he were gone on jazz; their voices contradicted Mother's down below, singing about Rosie Nell; Doc imitated Big Bill Broonzy, growling:

> *Michigan water tastes like cherry wine*
> *Mississippi water tastes like turpentine!*

Downstairs, Daddy was grumbling to Astrid about the young man coming so early in the day. "Boys," he said. "I don't like it a bit."

"There, there," she laughed at him. "More are coming during the week. Doc knows quite a few sheep breeders. You remember what you said: safety in numbers."

Astrid and Margo had spoken to Daddy while they all had mid-morning coffee at Margo's bed. He was making them a loan at three and a half percent. He'd have consented to any whim of the eldest when she lay there with that great new cast on her leg! Astrid phoned the man who owned the land, and it was as good as theirs. She was jubilant shouting up the stairs.

"Why don't you two hush up and listen to Mother."

From the busy kitchen, over the chatter of the help, the voice continued.

> *They often wished me with them*
> *But they always wished in vain!*
> *I'd rather be with Rosie Nell*
> *A-swinging in the lane.*

The phone jingled and Astrid's quick steps went down the hall to get it. "For you, baby," she called leaping up the steps to the room where they were.

"Who is it?" Kristin sat on the floor by Margo's bed, selecting another chocolate, one hand up on Bimbo.

"Answer and you'll find out." Astrid took Kristin's place.

Kristin went down, lazy. It was Danny. "And they want to pay you twenty-five dollars. You'll be on for ten minutes. You want to do it?"

"Okay. Yeah, I do."

"Someone'll be over with a truck to pick Blueberry up that morning. Don't forget; the second day of the fair."

"Yeah."

"Are your sisters going to bring their goats and rabbits?"

"Everything. And I have to show Margo's Nubians in the ring. Judging's tomorrow afternoon."

"Are you scared about the act?"

"I don't think so."

"Can she do that waltz I started?"

"She's slow. No."

"Well, I'll see you."

"So long, Danny."

Kristin went into the kitchen. "Mother."

"Well, dear?" Mother was kneeling by the oven taking out the fresh-baked bread, its perfume filling the room. She glanced up. "What is it?"

"I'm supposed to do a trick-horse act at the fair."

"Do you want to?"

"Yeah, I do."

"Well, that's nice. Is Blueberry ready for something like that? How will you ever get over there?"

"And I get paid. Wow." Stunned, Kristin walked out and upstairs to report. "I get money too," she told the three.

Doc was flattering. "The sheep barn boys are going to want an introduction. Particularly one Cheviot breeder."

Kristin blushed. "I'll go groom her, I guess, and decide what to do. Waltzing is out."

"Darn, I won't be able to see you," Margo said.

"Tell you what, I'll take a reel," Doc assured her. "I got a three-lens Sears camera."

"Please let me do your hair," Astrid begged. "And wear my new jeans, Kristin. And let her borrow your white silk shirt, Margo."

"You girls aren't going to have Kristin any more when you're done," Doc said. "Let her alone; she's different from you two."

"No." They turned on him, witheringly. "You think girls just happen!"

"My gosh, girls *work* on themselves."

"Thunderation. I take it back." Doc picked up his guitar:

I got the blues so bad it hurts my feet to walk;
Got the blues so bad it hurts my tongue to talk;
I got the blues so bad I just can't rest at night;
Got the blues so bad it's taken my appetite!

Kristin had already gone down to the paddock to tell the mare.

She and Astrid were up before dawn the next morning getting the milking and the chores out of the way. It was eight o'clock before they went rolling down Highway 12, the Ford pulling the trailer of stock, Astrid driving.

The sun shouted overhead and Kristin kept chattering about Blueberry until finally Astrid said, "Cut it out, baby, and let's start to think about the show ring this afternoon. When that's over you can talk all you want and I'll listen."

Kristin came down to earth. "Boy, I'm sorry!"

"They're judging Nubians at three o'clock. I didn't milk the does out thoroughly; I want them to have full bags for the ring."

"I really am sorry!"

"First thing," Astrid said, "help me unload the goats. Then you go find out where the small stock is supposed to be and get them settled."

"Okay."

Kristin had brought Teddy again. He was in Mr. Shams' carrying case under her knees. "I'm never going to be able to get a ribbon on him; he's always just on exhibit. Some time I wish someone else would bring in an Abyssinian guinea pig. For kicks."

"Maybe Teddy will get an Award of Merit this year."

"He ought to get a prize for traveling."

By the time Kristin had paid the entry fees and got every one in his proper cage, and when she had filled their water utensils and was heading back to the barn where Astrid was, it was late morning.

"Lead Sophie out," Astrid said, "I want to coach you some more on handling."

"Okay."

"Don't hug her. Stand away so the judge can see her conformation. Don't hold the collar so tight; it spoils her neck line. Don't hold her head so high; she's not a mule; make her look like a dairy animal. Set her feet where you want them; she won't move; I've worked on her. Keep her hind feet apart, one a little ahead of the other; that shows her udder to advantage. And her forehoofs side by side, distant enough so her nice deep brisket shows and she doesn't look narrow-chested."

"I'm a mess," Kristin worried. "I hope Danny doesn't come and watch."

But Astrid praised her. "You'll be okay I think."

"Darn. I don't know."

"I'll take the best entries in each class but you have to remember you can beat me just the same, baby. Judges all have their own ideas."

The goats wore their white stable coats with the green lettering, *Margastrid.* They fretted over the new quarters at first, and then settled down in the fresh yellow straw, accepting the tidbits of green and sliced turnips and anything Astrid could think up that they'd like. She even let Doc break cigarettes in two for them; half-aloof, half-curious, dainty, they chewed on the pieces of tobacco and paper.

"The sheep barn boys are coming to watch the judging. They're in the ring now, and soon it'll all be over for them."

"How are they doing?" Astrid said.

"Then I won't show." Kristin spoke flatly.

"What do you mean, baby?"

"I can't stand to be watched."

Doc said, "How about Blueberry? You'll have a crowd there."

"It's different. The goats aren't mine and I'm worried about doing right."

"I'll tell them to stay in their own barn," Doc said.

"Yeah!" Kristin sighed.

"How are you coming on her transformation?" he asked Astrid.

She winked at him. "Tonight. Blueberry won't recognize her."

"No," Kristin protested.

And then in mid-afternoon, despite Doc's word, there

were his sheep breeder friends, three of them, all college-age boys, swaggering on the ring edge, talking all during the Nubian judging so that Kristin was astonished when she was handed a Junior Champion ribbon on Queen. As she led her out, Astrid was approached by someone who wanted to put down a deposit on the next buck kid the new champion dropped. "I'd like to have it registered as Margastrid Queen's Rex," the new buyer said enthusiastically. "And I'll take any color that comes!" He handed Astrid a twenty dollar bill.

Kristin led Queen into her stall and put her white stable coat back on, fastening the little buckles. "Wow," she told Doc.

"Have you seen the sign, Kristin?" he asked.

"What sign?"

The sheep breeders were there hanging on the stall rails. "The one about your act," one said.

"That's why we asked Doc to let us meet you, beautiful," said the Cheviot breeder. "You're famous."

"We want to take you around and show you the fair."

"Will you let us!"

Kristin was confused. "Darn it. I guess so. If you don't mind stopping by the gypsy camp."

"We'll go where you go," they declared, reckless.

Astrid called, "Come on and take Pharaoh. The Two-Year-Old Buck Class is up."

One of the boys touched her braids as he opened the gate for her. "She's pretty, Doc."

"Don't get fresh with my girl," Doc told them.

"We'll meet you soon as the judging is over," the boys said. "Don't forget, Kristin!"

"Okay."

She showed Pharaoh, brown-and-tan-and-white mottled, snub-nosed, elegant with long curved ears. He took Best In Class, and would go up against the older bucks later for Best Buck In Show. There he lost, but she didn't mind, tacking up his lavender ribbon by Queen's purple rosette.

Finally, the four young men were showing Kristin and Astrid the entrance to the tall canvas tent where the animal acts would be shown. A fresh-painted sign listed the specialties, one reading: *Miss Kristin and Her Nationally Famous Trick Golden Buckskin Mare, Blueberry.*

"Now are you glad Astrid's going to do your hair over?" Doc asked.

Kristin smoothed her braids down. "I'll bet Danny cooked up that sign."

They went in back where the gypsies were, to inquire for him. "Hurry up, Kristin. We want to see the grounds."

They stayed behind her as she approached a young man with olive skin and black eyes who was in the shade in front of one of the scattered old house-trailers that had makeshift awnings of bright shawls or quilts that extended from their doors or shielded one side, under which were stools and tables and rugs.

The young man was reading a paperback novel and had a scraggly green parrot on his shoulder. "Danny isn't around, girlie."

"*Hola,*" said the parrot clearly. "I'm Pablo."

"He said to come here." Kristin knit her brows.

"He's busy with the *crayí.*"

"I'm going to meet your king. Danny told me I could."

The young man turned back to this book. "*Muy bien.* Go ahead. You won't like it. He eats little girls for breakfast. And his wife's a witch, you know."

The bird said, "I'm Pablo. *Hola.*"

"Come on," Doc said at her side. "We'll come back for Danny."

"Let's go see the side show, beautiful," a sheep breeder urged.

"Can I hold your bird?" Kristin stood over the young gypsy.

He grinned up and let the parrot walk onto her wrist. "Sometimes he bites, girlie. Watch him. He's old; I bet he's sixty years. He'll take a chunk right out of your arm."

Kristin told Doc, "Why don't all of you go on to the side show? I'll find you there in a little while."

"Where are your manners, baby," Astrid said. "You can't leave your dates."

"Who's a date?" Kristin ran her fingers over the colored feathers along the little bird's back. "I had a pet crow a while ago. And he's dead."

The gypsy said, "What happened?"

"Some darn possum or weasel got him."

"*Caramba.* What was he doing in the woods if he was a pet?"

"I don't know. I just had him there for a while."

"If you want to see Danny come tomorrow. He had to drive the horse van down into Illinois to pick up a few of our older colts. There's a rich buyer dickering with the *crayí* for them."

Kristin stroked the old bird's gnarled feet and it bent its head to watch, speechless, the yellow eyes following her movement, the huge crooked beak half-open. "I've got a horse act tomorrow afternoon."

"You're the one with the golden bucksin that's famous?"

"Yes, but she's not golden; her mane's black; that's made up."

"I might come to watch you, girlie."

"Okay." She gave him Pablo. "Will you tell him I was looking for him?"

"*Váyase.* Go along." Arrogant, his eyes returned to his book.

Kristin followed Astrid, one of the sheep barn boys on each side. "I don't think Danny wants to talk to me," she said.

"Why?" Astrid asked.

"And he doesn't want his dad to know he's here."

"Why?" Doc said.

"Maybe that gypsy would talk to him; Danny won't go back to school."

"Why?"

"*Váyase,*" she told them. "But I liked that gypsy."

"Sometime she acts like she's nine and a half years old, just like Daddy thinks she is," Astrid complained to Doc.

And that evening Margo said the same words to Mother. Astrid had put the littlest on the bench in Margo's bedroom and taken a scissors and made some bangs and brushed the rest back into a long pony tail. Astrid tied on a ribbon and handed Kristin a mirror.

"Ugh," Kristin said. "That's not me. I don't like it."

In the morning she came into Margo's room with her hair again in braids. "I refuse also to wear Margo's silk shirt," she stated. Except for the fringe of bangs Kristin was unchanged, tucking in the blue shirt that buttoned to the right like a man's that she got from the catalog, hitching up her pants and tightening her belt.

"Are you actually going to do an exhibition before people looking like that?" the eldest asked.

"No, I've got a white jersey in a bag with my brushes and groom rags; I'll change at the last minute. And I've got a couple of ribbons to tie on the braids. Are you satisfied? Leave me alone. *Caramba.* Yesterday I looked like a drip." Kristin was jumpy.

"Fame has gone to her head," Astrid said.

"No, Kristin's naturally stubborn," Margo claimed.

"I'm going down to the highway to watch for the truck. Blueberry's all ready," Kristin said. "I hope Danny's back."

"Aren't you scared?" Margo demanded.

The girl shrugged, dropping her eyes. "I don't think so."

Daddy came out to the drive where she stood looking. "Astrid says you were talking to gypsies."

"Astrid's a tell-tale," she flared, her blue eyes bright.

"You behave yourself. And mind your manners with those sheep friends of Doc's. Don't let them get fresh. You be a credit to your family." Daddy didn't hear what Kristin cried; he only scowled, wishing to mold her, to keep her a child at his side, wishing her to become a capable adult; Daddy strove with his emotions and his intelligence. "And don't speak to strangers."

"Okay."

A ramshackle three-quarter-ton truck was coming, the sides built high. The young olive-skinned gypsy was driving. "*Hola,* girlie!" he shouted.

"Where's Pablo!" she yelped, "*Hola.*" At home with the stranger of yesterday in a way she would never be with Daddy.

She dashed ahead of the truck leading him to the mare. When they reached the fair grounds Kristin was given a stall in the cattle-and-horse barn. Enormous Holstein bulls lowed, a pair of mares nickered back and forth, a great Brahma steer bellowed like a mule; the scent of offal and fresh field straw and hay and the sweating curried animals mingled in an intoxicating perfume; Draft Belgians clonked heavy shoes on the cement aisle-ways, men whistled and shouted and laughed.

The gypsy's dark eyes were sympathetic and before he left her, he watered Blueberry and showed Kristin the stack of hay that she could use. "You want a hot dog?"

"I wish Danny was here."

"He's sure to be back by afternoon. Let's get a hot dog."

"I don't want to leave her," Kristin said.

"Are you hungry?"

"I think so."

"What do you want on it?"

"Whatever they've got. Everything."

He brought toasted rolls and franks heaped with mustard and ketchup, two kinds of relish, green and red. They ate standing in the aisle, the food spilling over and onto the pavement. They rinsed their hands and mouths at a spigot, and the young man went away. "Good luck."

"Thanks."

Her uneasiness had begun, the stage fright that would continue to bother her until, seated on Blueberry, she would ride out and kneel to the crowd. Doc and the boys came to look at the horse and try to talk with Kristin. But she kicked at the side of the stall with rhythmical nervous sounds.

"I've got a stomach ache," she told Doc.

"What did you have for lunch?"

"I didn't; I had a hot dog for breakfast about eight."

"Come on."

"I'm not hungry." She got up and took the old bath towel to rub Blueberry down again.

"Will you eat some ice cream?"

"I don't think so."

He came back with a towering rainbow cone, six flavors. "Try it."

She finished it. "Do you think I could have another?"

And then it was almost two and she'd put on her white jersey top and dampened her hair at the water faucet, tied on the ribbons. She had been told where to wait in a dusty passageway. Under her, Blueberry sensed the tension and snorted, ready. Someone called out, "Go on in, miss!"

She heard the running feet padding up behind and turned. "*Hola*. Kristin!" It was him, his black curls tight, sunburned face flashing a white smile. He patted Blueberry's curved neck and slapped her flank as the voice called again.

"Can't you hear them announcing you? Snap to it!"

"Don't rush her," Danny cautioned.

"No."

Bareback, at a slow canter, she rode out before the bleachers. The mare reined in on a dime and bent to a knee, her mane flowing down silken. Kristin heard the loudspeaker saying her name; she saw Doc at the railing, the camera at his eye. She felt the unreality, the dream-like quality of the hour, the fantasy-girl and hero-horse; the fiction she'd used to make out of driftwood ridden in on waves, or the sled leaping under her down a sand dune, or the worn-out saddle in Danny's barn that was stored next to the fly-specked tattered posters, one of the black-haired girl and the eight running studs.

She moved Blueberry through her paces and tricks, the mare's coat dampening about the neck and then the flanks, foaming white between her muscular hind legs, and at her mouth. Blueberry moved sidewise in quick steps, facing the crowd; she reared and stood, seeming wild and out of control, and then up again on her hind legs, taking a few steps forward. She halted and Kristin slipped off her.

She told the mare to lie down and remain. She went away from her half the length of the stands. She turned and called, motioning Blueberry to sit. The horse rose to that position like a puppy, one hind leg tucked under her belly, the other casually sidewise, her forelock over her eyes, her expression ludicrous, so the crowd roared. Her gaze stayed on Kristin, who whistled her to come. The mare got to her feet and trotted, stopping on command, remaining where she was and rearing as Kristin flicked her hand.

Kristin turned away, going in the other direction from the mare. She dropped a handkerchief, not looking back. Blueberry hurried after to pick the cloth up and follow Kristin who paused and let her put it in her hand. The crowd clapped; the mare on signal bowed her head, nodding acknowledgment. Again the horse, dog-like, lay down. Kristin left her and went to the other end of the bleachers.

She glanced over at Doc and at the stands where the faces were a vague mixture of color and slight motion. She glimpsed Danny leaning against a pillar, his dark face triumphant. She turned and called and Blueberry scrambled to her feet, leaping, nickering, coming at a full charge and skidding to a stop, snorting.

"Hey, hey, girl." Kristin slipped on as the mare knelt, and then Blueberry again reared up, standing an instant with forelegs extended in a salute.

To a clapping from the stands, she rode from the ring at a collected canter, the horse's neck in an arch, the reins slack. In the aisle she dismounted. An envelope was thrust at her, "Your money, miss."

"Thanks."

"Some fellow's looking for you. I don't see him now. He was here just a minute ago."

"A black-headed boy? That's Danny. I'll wait."

"No. This guy was about sixty, miss. Gray hair and a big hat. I think he might be a cattle man. He wants to see you."

Up ahead, Danny and the gypsy were in the doorway to the tent in the bright sunlight. Pablo was on the young man's shoulder. As she approached, Blueberry trailing, he said, "Terrif, girlie."

"I like the way she stands and steps forward," Danny's eyes shone. "She's nice and strong; some mares can't do that."

"Yeah!"

"Meet my friend here and his crazy bird. *Caramba.*"

"He told me your king eats people for breakfast and the queen's a witch."

"Have you two met?"

"I hauled her nag over this morning," the young gypsy said. "And yesterday she was looking for you. I've got to take you back home too, girlie."

"When?" Kristin asked. "Can you wait a while?"

"I'm not on till the night show. It's up to you."

"*Hola,*" said Pablo.

"*Hola* yourself," Danny said. "Let's take Kristin to see the king."

"*Muy bien.* I hope he's not asleep."

"Can I see your horses too?"

"Maybe you can," said the gypsy. "We don't let outsiders in very often."

"But Danny's my friend. That's where I learned to train my horse."

"I recognized that handkerchief trick, girlie."

"They use that one all the time," Danny said.

"Do they!"

The afternoon sun moved above the fair grounds like a slow cannonball. The three strode to the horse enclosure, Blueberry trotting behind. They tied her outside. "She's a stranger, girlie, and we don't allow a new horse in with our crowd till it's ready. We don't tie our *caballos* up and they don't wear any rigs on them unless they're working. Our horses are our children."

They stood at the round paddock, shaded by branches laid in a kind of latticework overhead, where the horses milled. The little green parrot climbed solemnly on Kristin's wrist, and the young men called the animals over. The beasts crowded, affectionate, wanting the hands on them, the voices in their ears.

"They're used to hand-grooming, girlie. Ever hear that the best way to clean an oil painting by one of the masters is with the palm of your hand? Same with horses."

"The darlings."

Danny's voice was soft, "Hey, hey, little horses."

"Let's go see if the *crayi*'s awake," the gypsy said.

While the three walked, Kristin brought up the subject again. "But you *ought* to go back to school."

"Why? I don't need it."

They came to where the trailers were in the dry hot grass. Before one on a folding iron First World War army cot slept the *crayi*, a folded dirty red quilt for a pillow, an oriental rug over his legs and one on the grass by him. "*Allí está*," said the young gypsy, "there he is."

Kristin walked between them, Pablo on her shoulder, his claws on her now-soiled jersey. "Shhh."

"No." Danny was bold. "Come on, Kristin."

They stopped before the olive-hued man whose hair

was black and heavy like a child's, and who wore a single gold earring. His ruddy face was covered with a three-day bristle; his high cheekbones were cavernous, his frame, once a full six-foot-three, had shrunk with age. He opened an eye, large and dark, and closed it again; his lips were petulant. "*Quien es?*"

"Speak English, old man," Danny told him.

Both eyes opened. "Who's that?" The expression was malignant. His eyes closed again, his large mouth surly. "I want my *vino. Donde esta mi arroz?* I am tired."

The young gypsy clapped his hands and a pair of small boys came out of another trailer with the king's wine and a pot of hot yellowed rice. "We must go away while he eats. Let's wait over here, girlie."

"He's eighty-three years old," Danny said.

"Who's king after he dies?" Kristin said.

"They haven't figured about that yet. He'll live to be a hundred and ten."

"Wow."

The *crayi* was whining, and the little boys ran back to the trailer, clapping their hands. "*Rèina, rèina,*" they shouted.

A woman came from the trailer carrying a guitar. She was slender and well-formed, walked like a dancer, throwing back the purple fringed shawl about her shoulders. Her hair was jet, blue-glinted in the sun like the crow Smoky had been. She glanced at the three as she walked past to the old man's cot. Her large earrings swung and she made a gesture toward them, half-snarling, her white teeth flashing.

"*Dona María,*" Danny said. "His wife. Those were his great-great grandsons."

"A witch," the young man told Kristin. "Who knows how old the queen is? Eighty, at least."

"*Caramba.*" Kristin said the new word easily. "Wow."

The woman had seated herself on the oriental rug on the ground, and was singing, hoarse and low-pitched. When she had done the man said, "*Malagueña.*"

And she began to play again, complying. At last, seeing him put his empty dish aside, she rose. She cast another suspicious look upon the trio, silent, sweeping by to disappear.

"*Muy bien.* Come on, now."

The king, on an elbow, held his long-stemmed crystal glass. "Tell me what you think of us *gitanos?*"

The green bird was preening on her shoulder. Kristin flushed. "I always knew this *gitano* here." She nudged Danny. "He's my best friend."

"So?" He motioned in the direction of the trailer. "Will you join me in *té?*"

"No thanks."

"*Pronto,*" he told the young gypsy who ran off. "Now what is it you wish of me?"

"She just wants to meet you, old man," Danny said.

"No, that's not so, king," Kristin said. "I came to ask you to make him go home to his dad."

"But he's not gypsy and Danny's mother was. We can use Danny with our carnival."

"You gave your niece permission to marry Mr. Wasilewski. So that means he was a nice man. He's Polish."

"That's so; I did." He laughed aloud, sharp, his mouth wide amid his white teeth; two gold ones and in them diamonds sparkling. The ring in his ear glinted.

"He ought to go to school," she said. "He hated it when he left. He told me he did."

"I won't, Kristin," Danny warned.

"And I'm even going to veterinary college, king. That's what I'm going to make my life work."

"It won't do any good," Danny said.

"Kindly be quiet," the *crayí* told Danny, "while the *señorita* and I are having conversation. Ah, *muy bien*." The silver tray had arrived. It held a tall glass decanter of a dark liquid, and there were thick glasses to hold the tea. The old man bent to pour each half full. "Now we will toast. And Danny will go back where he belongs for the present. If when he has finished his school, he wishes to come with us, we will have a place for him. I could wish him to marry back into his tribe. But I'm afraid he will let his eyes fall elsewhere."

The children took the glasses and touched the heavy rims together. "Toast to you," Kristin said quietly. "Cheers, king."

"You must say it our way, girlie, when you are visiting," the young man told her. "*Salud*."

"*Salud*," said the old man, gloomy, "*Retejos parchandrá, sos cayicó flacha sinará*."

"He says today is the carnival," the gypsy translated, "but tomorrow there will be only ashes."

"Ugh," Kristin said, "*salud* anyway." She sipped the strong bitter liquid.

The *crayí*'s eyes closed, half-sleepy. "He'll let his eyes fall on blue ones. And how do you like us *gitanos*? Did I ask you that before?"

"I'm crazy about gypsies," Kristin told him, "and Danny taught me a lot of things."

"His mother was one of our best girls; she spoke horse better than English."

"I know," Kristin said.

"Danny was the one insisted on us billing that act you

put on out there. He even told the painter what to put on the poster."

"Why'd you make it so fancy, Danny?"

"Kristin," Danny sounded angry, "I don't want to go home."

"You'll do what the old *crayí* tells you," the man said. He looked at Kristin, his expression changing from that of a kindly old man to a surly one. "*Váyase.*"

The young man adjusted his pillow and the king laid back on it. "Let's go, girlie."

The king chanted, "We gypsies are a poor lot; we have nothing."

The young man winked at Kristin, "It's too bad."

"We are evil; we curse all mankind; we're a lot of beggars, a worthless king and a witch for a queen. We have nothing but our pride:

> *El Italiona pide cantando*
> *El Francés Ilorando,*
> *El Gitano regañando!*"

He closed his cruel mouth. "*Váyase.* Go away."

As they put down their glasses and went, Kristin cried, "What was he saying?"

"He says Italians beg with a song, Frenchmen with a tear, and us with a growl." The young man laughed.

"I hate to leave him." Kristin's fingers caressed the toes of the little parrot. I even hate to leave Pablo."

"Keep him, girlie. He's yours."

"No."

"Take the place of that crow the weasels caught."

"Smoky?" Danny was startled.

"Yeah."

"I hate that," Danny said, frowning. "I'd get another crow first chance."

"That's what I thought I'd do."

"And teach him what Smoky knew," Danny said darkly. "So it'd be as if he never died."

When they got to Blueberry the young gypsy said, "*Adios*. When you get ready to take the mare home, let me know."

"Wish you lived around here," Kristin said. "*Adios, gitano.*"

He was gone and Danny said, "I don't like your speaking up to the king like that, Kristin."

"You have to do what's right, Danny." She knit her brows. "Like your mother said: do good and you'll feel good; do bad and you'll feel bad."

"No." He denied the girl.

A tall graying man in a big Stetson was bearing down upon them, his voice booming. "Hey, miss! I've been all over this carnival looking for you."

"Why?"

Her parrot looked at the man. "*Hola.* I'm Pablo."

The man reached a finger out and the bird snatched for it, catching the end. The man shook the pinched member, towering over the children. "Well, that's the nicest little bareback horse act I ever saw, miss. Where'd she learn those tricks?" He looked Blueberry up and down.

"Why? From me."

"Well, here's the way it is; I got a proposition if you're willing. How'd you like to take a couple of colts for me and train them like that; think you could?"

Kristin reddened. "*Caramba.*"

"Teach them tricks; pay you a hundred and fifty a season and board."

"Dollars?" Kristin said.

"See, I run a classy little guest farm over in Ohio and

I got nothing in the stable but the cream. That's the way
I run the place. Now I been looking for an angle, and
when I saw you down there without a saddle, a little kid
with braids and that dirty white shirt, I thought, let's go."

"Wow," Kristin told Danny, "wait till I tell Margo."

"Where'd you pick that up, miss? I was bowled over
by your precision and the way nothing went wrong."

"From Danny." She nodded toward the boy who stood
back from them.

"This Danny?"

"Yes, sir."

"Maybe you'd take a couple too for me. Same arrange-
ment: fee and send me the feed and bedding bills. I'll be
responsible. You interested?" He thrust out a huge hand
and shook the boy's.

"Okay," Danny said.

"Double luck for me," the man said. "Let me have your
phone numbers, kids. I've traded for a few colts here at
the fair. Maybe you could take them right away. Got any
place to put them?"

"We'll use my dad's old shed," Danny said.

"Did you buy the *caballos* from the gypsies here?"
Kristin asked.

He shook his head and pursed his mouth, wise. "Take
it from me, miss. Look out for them."

"I know," Kristin said.

"I thought I'd get knifed while we were dealing.
Gypsies are a mean breed, whining and complaining one
minute, and the next growling and ready to fight. They're
a lot of paupers, all of them, but they think they're a bunch
of royalty. I even heard there's a king that travels with them
somewhere."

"Don't believe everything you hear," Kristin said.

"I felt the hex on me," he said. "But I liked these three-year-olds so much I stuck it out; they're beauts. They brought them in this morning. Set me back a penny, too. These people know horses; they breed the best. But they drive a hard bargain. You'd think they were selling one of their children."

Danny was straight-faced. "Never trust a gypsy."

"Don't let them find out which pocket your billfold's in either!" Kristin patted Pablo.

The big man rubbed his index finger. "And watch out for that parrot, miss. He's got a touch of meanness."

"Okay," she giggled.

That evening the young gypsy drove Danny and Kristin and Blueberry home in the ancient truck. They turned the mare into her paddock and locked Pablo in Smoky's cage on the barn wall. Then they went over to the Wasilewski place. The young man waited in the truck's cab while the two children went to stand at the front door.

"Danny's back," Kristin said.

The stooped man ran his thick-jointed hands over his bald head, half-embarrassed. "I sold off three-quarters of this farm for money, Danny."

The boy grinned. "I heard you were sort of rich."

"I was afraid you wouldn't come back when you knew I was getting along so well. I thought you'd wander around till you found some of your mother's people to take you in."

"No," Danny said. "I like it fine with you."

"I'm painting the house," his dad said. "First inside and then out. Figure to fix the place up a little."

"It won't take long with him home," Kristin said. "Could we use that old carriage house to keep some horses in?"

"Use anything you like," Mr. Wasilewski said, his

eyes on his son. "Have you got taller? Or do I just remember you when you were a little boy?"

"I'm taller."

"How'd you like my brother, Jock?"

"He's all right," Danny said, "except he's pretty free with his belt strap if you speak up."

"Jock's not mean," Mr. Wasilewski said, turning to Kristin. "He just thinks everyone's the same as he is. My brother's lived alone on that Holstein cow farm too long."

"Yeah," Danny said.

"Your mother comes over now and then," he told Danny, "around the lunch hour."

"Does she still do that?" Kristin said.

"Just to be sure my dad's all right," Danny said, "and to see if everything's okay. And here I am back; I guess she sent me."

"And I'll paint the carriage house too," Mr. Wasilewski said. "I'll put a big picture of a nag on it if you like, the way us Poles like to do. We're in favor of lots of color. And we like noise too. It's been quiet here."

"Not any more," Danny said. "Let's go."

They dashed out to the carriage house and took brooms to the heavy dust and spider webs that draped from the rafters and the windows and in the corners. They dusted off the fading posters, the one of the young *gitana* and her eight rushing black stallions. Danny, with the gypsy's help, wheeled the rusty farm machines, a toothed harrow and a hay rake, creaking, into the yard. The unused dirt floor was spongy and must-scented.

Then the two young men dropped Kristin off and they returned to the fair. In the van, Danny, with the other's help, brought over the colts; a lanky iron gray, a small-boned blue roan and two black matched fillies. Danny knew each and its name, leading it down the shaky tail-gate and turning it into the barn room, unhaltered.

"Hey, hey, little horses," they crooned.

The gypsy climbed up into the van that groaned as he pressed the starter. "I'll be seeing you, Danny."

"*Adios.*" Danny waved as he rumbled away.

The boy went into the shed, turning to the gleaming beasts who crowded near, alarmed by their strange surroundings. After a while Kristin cantered up on Blueberry, the green bird riding her wrist. She came in the doorway, Blueberry gazing over her shoulder to the big colts and the boy who stood in the midst of them.

"Wow," she said. "*Hola.*"

He grinned. "And pretty soon you have to quit riding your nag, Kristin."

"I know."

Shining, their eyes met over the five horses, six counting the one that stirred now in the dark place, its color and nature unknown until it would unfold in the spring.